T0106217

Links

A Short Story Collection

Kaylia M. Metcalfe

iUniverse, Inc.
New York   Bloomington

Links
A Collection of Connection

This is a work of fiction. All of the characters, names, incidents, organizations, and dialogue in this novel are either the products of the author's imagination or are used fictitiously.

iUniverse books may be ordered through booksellers or by contacting:

iUniverse
1663 Liberty Drive
Bloomington, IN 47403
www.iuniverse.com
1-800-Authors (1-800-288-4677)

Because of the dynamic nature of the Internet, any Web addresses or links contained in this book may have changed since publication and may no longer be valid. The views expressed in this work are solely those of the author and do not necessarily reflect the views of the publisher, and the publisher hereby disclaims any responsibility for them.

ISBN: 978-1-4401-7185-7 (sc)
ISBN: 978-1-4401-7186-4 (ebk)

Printed in the United States of America

iUniverse rev. date: 9/17/2009

Contents

Acknowledgments

When I sat down to write a short story collection, I had no idea how much work was going to be involved. I would like to think that had I known ahead of time what undertaking this project would entail, I would have started it earlier in life. Chances are I might have let fear overwhelm desire, and I might have put off starting it until that ever elusive "later."

Regardless, this book would not have been possible without the help, guidance, and cheerleading antics of a whole bunch of very special people.

Thank you to my blog readers, my former English teachers (especially Mrs. Williams, Mrs. Rystad, and Dr. Mackey), my family, and my long-suffering friends. Thank you for putting up with me.

Special thanks to:

Stephanie, for the cover art and bio photos.

Jessica, for the Web page and the occasional dose of reality served over sushi.

Leah, for being the first person to look me straight in the eye and tell me to be a writer.

My amazing editor, Monika, for her unwavering support, attention to detail, patience, and determination that I learn the proper use of commas.

Matthew, for his encouragement, words of wisdom, faithful support, and unwavering faith that I could actually do this.

I am honored to be linked to each and every one of you.

For

Kristen

And

Gina

Introduction

There are more than 6 billion people on this planet, and half of them live in my city. Well, that's an exaggeration, but it feels true. The number is actually closer to 7.2 million and growing every day, which is still a lot of people to cram together, even into a place as big as the San Francisco Bay area.

Growing up in the forty-eighth-largest urban center of the world gives you a unique perspective on things. Concepts like *crowded* and *traffic* have inherently different meanings to me and my neighbors than they do for my relatives living in the Midwest.

And yet, I have also been lucky enough to travel to places that make this part of California look small, even downright quaint.

But no matter the size of the urban sprawl, I have learned that people are just people. Whether they are stacked up on top of each other in teeny-tiny apartments that reach for the Tokyo sky or nestled in prairie homesteads separated by miles of farmland, people are still ... just people.

And part of what makes people so interesting is how they connect to one another. No, I don't mean the

Kevin Bacon way of connection (although that's mighty interesting). I mean the personal connection, the series of shared moments and the small things that add up to big bonds.

I call them links.

We want to be linked to others … we want others to be linked to us. That primal urge that made us gather around the fire to tell stories of past adventures is the same motivation that leads groups of giggling twelve-year-old girls to swap makeup kits and thirty-year-old men to argue football plays on Monday mornings. We are a species that thrives on being linked to one another, and we will use all of our tools in order to make it happen. There are blogs and message boards, barstools and mixers, clubs for every possible hobby or thrill, dating sites, and, possibly most prevalent of all, religion. In the end, they all feed the same desire.

Getting linked.

But … life isn't easy; simply desiring a connection in no way guarantees its existence. That's where this book comes from. In the following ten short stories, you will find the age-old refrain of people very much like you and me, who are trying to make or keep a connection. Some of them manage. Some of them fake it, hoping that someday it will be real. They are not allegorical or epic stand-ins for great and lofty ideals … they are just people (like your noisy neighbor, the woman in front of you in line at the post office, the guy who tailgated you last weekend on the freeway). They are just simple people who are caught up in the complex and universal dance of striving to connect.

Sometimes they succeed. Many times they fail. They keep trying.

In a world with 6 billion people, it's all we can do.

Kaylia Metcalfe
June 2009

Angel

He was standing against the building, leaning back in a well-practiced posture of patience, when the woman with the pigtails left the store. Like the hundreds of other shoppers he had seen that night, there was nothing remarkable about her.

Now, the lady ten minutes before, on the other hand, the one wearing what looked like a robe and curlers in her hair as if she had been magically transported out of time or had decided to shop in a bad Halloween costume, she had been something worth noticing. Angel would have bet the forty-six bucks in his left jeans pocket that she had ice cream in her bags, and he hadn't bothered with her. You got to where you knew what people were going to say before you even asked. A lot of the time, he didn't even bother.

When he did ask, no matter the attitude with which he was rejected, he always followed up with a kind word. His buddies made fun of him for this. They preferred to either throw insults or simply move on to the next potential soft heart, but Angel had this crazy notion that someday someone would be so moved by his "That's okay, God bless you anyway" line, that they would turn around and give him something. He knew it was stupid, and after two years of working the doors of Walgreens, Targets, and Save Marts, it hadn't worked. But he did it anyway. He told Little Mike it was part of a social experiment—that handling was all about the social experiment—and, of course, the cash. He knew better than to tell the other guys that.

Last summer, a woman actually walked back to him after his benediction, and he had felt a spark of hope, of excitement. She hadn't been in a charitable mood, however, and had instead spent the next ten minutes lecturing him about God. Remaining calm had been difficult. He had finally gotten fed up with the bitch and slipped from his "I am respectful" street voice into his deeper "respect me" street voice and told her to move on. The switch was unconscious, he liked to tell himself, but there had been a moment while she was walking away—shoulders back, nose in the air—that he had wanted to smash her face into the ground, ram her perfectly painted skin into the asphalt, and grind the dirt into her pores. Instead, he lit another cigarette.

For the most part, people either ignored him completely or mumbled something about "Not carrying cash." A few would add "Sorry," which always seemed more instinctual than apologetic. Occasionally, an older person (usually a man) would get in his face and tell him to get a job. Angel hated those guys the worst; so arrogant, as if they knew anything about anything.

Handling wasn't his only job. He had a regular gig loading and unloading trucks at the FedEx hub. But that job didn't pay shit, and besides, handling let him hang with the guys and avoid home. Angel knew that he was lucky; he didn't really need the cash, and a part of him even felt a little guilty. Every night he would tell himself, "Tonight is the last night," but then the next day he would be out there, hands in his pockets so he wouldn't look threatening to the suburban housewives.

"Hey, got any spare change?"

A mumbled response, and a few minutes later it would repeat.

Like every other night this week, tonight had started out the same. He had met up with Ro and Ben after work and then headed over here to stand in the bright glow of this Walgreens store and waste time until later. *Later* was a concept as old as the idea of change, and Angel felt that it just about summed up everything. He would get a better job, *later*. He would call his mom, *later*. He would figure out what to do about the money he owed Little Mike, *later*. Hell, *later* was so big that it could be everything. Leaving *now* to just be one moment after another. Angel was okay with that while he was at work or out shooting pool, or drinking. He was even okay with that while asking people for money. It was when he was alone, in the crappy studio apartment with the leaky shower faucet and the stains on the walls, that the thought of how *later* was really *now* and *now* was yesterday's *later* would start to eat away at him. But, like Little Mike always said, "That's why there's booze."

Booze was later. Now was leaning, asking, and then trying to force apathy when they kept walking. That was until the woman with the pigtails. They weren't high, bouncy pigtails; she looked too old for that. They were just long, hanging pigtails, practically touching her chin, with the rubber bands knotted up high. She was carrying a bag in each hand, chewing her bottom lip, and her eyes were already scanning the parking lot. This was a woman in a mild hurry, and he hesitated. Two bags meant less likely; distracted meant less likely. But she was a woman, and she had laugh lines and pigtails; for some reason, he thought she might be nice.

"Hey, ma'am, got any spare change tonight?"

She shook her head slightly and looked down, moving past him and stepping off of the curb.

"That's okay. God bless you anyway."

He said his line dutifully and had already turned back to the door when he realized that she had stopped walking. She turned back to look at him, in her eyes a flicker of … something Angel couldn't quite place. She didn't look angry, just surprised. He pushed himself away from the wall and stood up straight.

She shifted the bags and walked back to him, digging in her pocket with her free hand. He heard the sound of loose change as she pulled out a handful. She glanced down but didn't bother to count the coins.

He bent forward and let her pour the assortment of change into his palm. From the corner of his eye, he took a closer look at her. She was youngish, around his age, somewhere in her late twenties. Her jacket was old, and her jeans were stained and fraying at the cuffs. Her fingers were covered in tiny cuts; her nails were all bitten down to the quick.

"Thank you, thank you," he said, feeling suddenly embarrassed. She nodded, turned, and walked away with her head down. Once again, she stepped off the curb.

"Hey, wait." He stood there with his hands partially outstretched, full of the change. Part of his mind was wondering how odd it was that the coins were so warm against his palms. Another part of his brain wanted to tell her somehow that he had been waiting for his line to work, that this was a big deal, a pivotal moment. She turned back, her face a question, and that was when the minivan hit her.

Later, Angel would tell the cops, his friends, his mother on the phone, anyone who would listen, that he hadn't seen the minivan until it was too late. He would tell them that it had been dark, that the asshole driver hadn't had his headlights on, that everything slowed down, and that in the split second it took for him to breathe in, there had been a *thud* that echoed. And then she was gone.

He ran forward; all he could hear was the sound of the change hitting the sidewalk. The minivan (some dark color with a scratch on the driver's door he would tell people later) was poised over her, and he could see that most of her was underneath, her bags tangled around her arm, and her jacket pushed up. In the dark, the colors swam together. Was that her T-shirt or a flash of skin? He bent over her, his body draping everything in shadows and tried to see.

She wasn't moving. Angel got down on his knees against the bumper of the minivan and leaned over her, blinking rapidly to try to see how much of her was underneath.

Suddenly, he reeled back, his hands covering his face. The driver had turned on his headlights, and all at once, the ground was bright and glowing. It was like a switch had been flipped and he could hear again: people yelling, the hum of the minivan's engine, his own ragged breath.

There was an argument behind him, and someone started cursing. In his ears there was a dull roar. In the light he could finally see the blood.

"Get back, get back. Someone call 911." It was him yelling, but he wasn't paying attention. Surely someone else had said the same thing. "Get back!" he cried again, even as a quick glance showed him that though a small crowd had gathered on the sidewalk near the door, no one else had moved beyond the florescent glow of the pharmacy lights. He was the only one.

Angel tried to think … what should he do? What could he do? She was lying face down, her body twisted, her arms outstretched. There was blood coming from her head, and her legs were still underneath the minivan somewhere. He tilted his head and blinked; the whole thing had a misplaced crooked view as if he were looking at it all from an angle.

He heard the minivan's engine rev. The headlights shifted, and with an explosion of air, it drove backward. There was a collective gasp from the audience, and it took Angel a moment to realize why. The van had still been *on* her, it had been on her leg, on her waist, and that was why everything was crooked. As the minivan pulled back, the headlights bounced down and now everyone could see what Angel had been seeing.

Good, he thought, get off her, now turn on your brights so we can see how bad it is … but the driver didn't turn on his brights. Instead, the minivan kept backing up farther and farther until there was no more headlight glow at all. Then, in a squeal of tires, it tore across the parking lot and barreled into traffic. Honks and yells followed in its wake, but ten seconds later it was gone. Suddenly, everything got quiet.

He turned accusingly to the crowd. "Did someone call 911?" A few people nodded; a few people looked away. No one was looking at her. She moved then, just a tiny turn of the head and the tiniest of moans. Angel let out a breath he hadn't known he had been holding.

He got down on the ground gently, oh so gently, and pushed her hair away from her face. In the semidarkness he could see one of her eyes. It was open, gazing at something only she could see. He stared at it, overcome, and then jumped slightly when she blinked.

"Hey." He lowered his voice and tried to keep as much of the street out of it as possible. "Hey there, lady, you okay? Yeah, you're okay. The paramedics are coming, no problem, you're fine."

She blinked at him again.

"It was nothing," he babbled on, moving her hair off her face, shocked at the intimacy of touching her but not knowing what else to do. "You're a little squished, but you're fine, can you breathe okay? Don't try to talk; it's gonna be okay."

The crowd on the sidewalk murmured.

Her eye was brown. No, he told himself, both eyes were brown. She still had two, but it just didn't feel like there was more to her anymore. He didn't want to think about anything else but her eye and the fact that it was locked onto him and blinking.

"Don't worry. It's gonna be okay." Was he lying? He didn't know, didn't want to think about it. She had nice eyelashes.

When Angel was ten, his grandmother had died. Being the kind of woman she was, she had decided to die at home. She had said it was so that there would be less work later, but Angel's mother had sworn that the old bitch had died at home so that they could all be part of the drama. His mother got a lot of mileage out of the story of his grandmother's death; it was the kind of story that got you pity or compassion or even laughter when told just right. Being the kind of woman she was, Angel's mother had made the story a bit more dramatic with each retelling.

Angel had been enlisted by his mother for the "death watch," a notion that had terrified him. With his cousins, he took turns sitting on a small chair next to his grandmother's bed and waiting. Sometimes she was awake and she talked, telling long rambling stories of her girlhood in the South, or of all the bastards who had tried to take advantage of her, or of neighborhood gossip about people long dead. Other times, she slept, and the unfortunate watcher had to lean in close to check her breathing, almost touching her papery skin that smelled like sickness. Her breath was so shallow that at times she didn't appear to be breathing at all. Once, Angel was sure that she had died as he sat in the darkened room listening to the clock tick and the far-off sounds of his cousins playing. He had been just about to call out for his mother when suddenly her eyelashes quivered and she drew a ragged breath.

Now, Angel watched as the eyelashes around the woman's light brown eye fluttered. She kept blinking long blinks, and he realized that she must be struggling to stay conscious. He snapped his fingers inches away from her face, hating the harshness but feeling relief when she focused back on him.

"You have to stay with me." And then he couldn't think of anything else to say. Absently, he picked up her hand and was surprised when her fingers gripped his.

"Hey now, see, no problem, you're okay…. You even get to hold my hand. Lucky you, eh?" She blinked.

It had been years since he had held anyone's hand. In fact, he couldn't remember the last time. Her hand was small, her fingers calloused. Absently, he rubbed his fingers over the grooves in her skin and kept talking, using his happy street voice, the one he used with cashiers and waitresses and middle aged bus drivers.

"So, where were you going? Huh? Going home? Just picking up some groceries right? Then home? Well, you'll be home soon enough…. And look, your bags are right here, see … I got 'em." He pulled the white plastic bags toward him, letting the loud crinkle sound distract him for a moment. Absently, he opened the one on top and rummaged inside.

"Look, we got your dried fruit, gross. We got your deodorant. We got your shampoo…."

It seemed wrong to see her personal things like that; he felt his cheeks flush. He pushed everything back into the bag and shoved it toward the curb. Lying down on the asphalt, he put his face as close as he dared to hers. "It's going to be okay." He was embarrassed by the tremble in his voice. In the distance he could hear the whine of sirens. He squeezed her hand again.

When he dreamt about it later (regularly, for the rest of his life), the dreams always started at that moment when he squeezed her hand. The dream version of her would squeeze back, then push up from the ground, and she would stand up. She would smile up at him, and he would become aware that he was still holding her hand. The dream would change then. Sometimes, she would be with him in his grandmother's bedroom, holding his hand, comforting him, waiting with indrawn breath for the flutter of eyelashes. Other times, she would simply smile at him and then walk away through the parking lot, swinging her grocery bags as she disappeared into the darkness.

He would wake up, and for a long moment, he would allow himself the luxury of the dream; he would imagine how she looked, both bags in one hand and the other pulling all her spare change out and giving it to him. He didn't like to think about what happened later.

Standing against the wall near the automatic door, he watched over the shoulder of the interviewing cop as they loaded her onto the gurney and lifted her up off the ground. The cop was some hard-ass who looked to Angel like he should be auditioning for the role of "Football Player Number Three" in a high school play. He kept leaning into Angel, blocking his view, and Angel kept moving over ever so slightly so he could watch the paramedics. He felt that if he looked away for even a moment, he would be betraying her in some way. It wasn't until the harsh sound of the zipper and the finality of her being completely hidden from him that he actually looked the cop (Officer Plancet) in the eye.

No, he couldn't identify the driver; no, he didn't see which direction the minivan went; yes, he was sure there was a scratch on the driver's side door; yes, he was positive that the headlights hadn't been on; no, she hadn't been running through the parking lot; no, he didn't know her.

But that last part was a lie, and as Angel climbed into Little Mike's beat up Ford an hour later, he thought about it. He didn't know her name, but he knew her. He felt that he could have told Officer Plancet all about her, how she was kind and generous and tired, how her hands were calloused, and how beautiful her eye had been.

"Let me buy you a drink." Little Mike's solution to everything. Angel slumped in the passenger seat with his head against the window and knew he didn't have the energy to argue. A few blocks later they pulled over, and Little Mike bought multicolored bottles that promised peace masquerading as temporary oblivion. The cashier wrapped them unceremoniously in brown paper while talking to Little Mike in that loud respectful way that all liquor store cashiers had. The light glared off their skin, and watching from the car, Angel thought that they weren't really there at all, not people, just reflected light.

On the floorboard were the shopping bags. No one had asked him if they belonged to her, and Angel hadn't known exactly what to do with them. It seemed wrong to leave them on the curb as if their owner had simply wandered off and might come back later. He could have given them to the frazzled EMT who, while making a quick detour into the Walgreens to stock up on Red Bull and chewing gum, had left the back doors of the rig open, letting the crowd get one final look before they drove away. But he hadn't wanted to. What would happen to them anyway? Some morgue staff person would probably pick through them, take anything worthwhile, and throw the rest away. He couldn't imagine that her family or friends would care about the shampoo or the fruit.

He got out of the car, surprised that he wasn't colder, that he could still feel the air on his arms and care. Around the back of Lou's Liquors he found the dumpster, and with one heave he tossed both plastic bags in. They made a soft thud as they hit the other trash, and then it was silent again. He got back in the car and sat still and upright, his seat belt on for the first time since he was a teenager. Little Mike opened the driver's door and handed over the bottles.

"Okay, got some stuff, Lou in there says that Rattler is playing downtown tonight." Angel said nothing. Little Mike put the key in and then glanced over.

"Look man, don't worry. It's okay. You'll feel better later."

Angel nodded, and the car pulled away from the curb.

Aside

We are driving down Stevens Creek Boulevard, the sun shining in our eyes and the music turned up loud enough to curtail any type of meaningful conversation. Suddenly, she slams on the brakes, jolting me out of my semidrowsy state. In the instant that it takes for me to realize that some idiot driver in a red Ford Escort almost hit us, I become aware of something altogether more unsettling. In the flash of action, she had thrown her right arm in front of me.

I take a deep breath and try not to think of the role reversal.

A moment later, her hands are safely on the steering wheel, and we are back in the steady stream of traffic as if nothing has happened. I shift in my seat, glancing at her and trying to figure out which bothers me more, her instantaneous impulse that should have been mine or the silence now because I didn't know how to respond to it.

What had been courteous and natural now seems somehow forced. I can see her glancing at me out of the corner of her eye as she maneuvers her Jeep through traffic. We speed through the Saratoga Avenue intersection in a blur, and then without warning, she pulls the car over and stops on the side of the road, front tire ever so slightly on the curb.

I look around, unsure, "Where are we?"

She sighs and turns off the radio. The car is in park now, hazard lights blinking, shaking as the other cars pass by. I become pointedly distracted by the "Happy Italian Food" sign, and only after the silence begins to stretch out to an uncomfortable length do I realize that she hasn't bothered to answer my question. She isn't looking at me. She is staring out the front window, her eyes unseeing.

"Hey, you okay?"

I am mildly concerned, unsure if we are about to have some sort of talk or if she is just working her way through something. Maybe both. I consider reaching out to touch her, but I don't know how. In the three weeks since our first awkward meeting at the Flames Coffee Shop where we shook hands, we haven't touched.

"What are we doing?" It is she who asks this question, and for a moment, I am annoyed because it really seems to be the sort of thing that I should be asking. She repeats herself but doesn't look at me.

"Well, we are sitting in the car not getting any closer to dinner." I am trying to make light of the situation because suddenly I know where this is going, and it scares me.

She turns and looks at me, full on in that frank and open way that has always slightly unnerved me, and I suddenly remember the first time I saw her.

She had been so tiny, had weighed practically nothing, although they had assured me that she was a healthy six pounds. How anything could be healthy at only six pounds was beyond me, but I had checked her over myself, carefully unwrapping the blanket and looking in wonder at her tiny fingers and toes. Throughout my inspection, she had lain still and gazed up at me, her eyes seeming too big for her head. As the years passed and she grew, her eyes never really changed. From her baby blanket she had regarded me with the same look she is wearing now, part question, part challenge. I hadn't known what to do with her then, and all these years later, I still don't. Dinner seems a long way off.

She just sits there with her open unblinking eyes and her unfulfilled expectations. I know it's my turn; I know that she is waiting, but my inner child doesn't want to volunteer anything or make it any easier for her. If she wants an actual answer, then she is going to have to ask an actual question. This is years of bitterness that she isn't responsible for. I know I am punishing her for my own past mistakes, and even though I feel shame at this realization, I can't bring myself to say anything, not yet.

I can't match her look for intensity, and I turn away ashamed and look out the window. Over the rooftops of San Jose, the sun is setting. I can see it now, a disc of untold radiance, hovering. If I stay quiet and still, I will be able to watch it disappear behind the buildings. I wish I could join it.

When she finally speaks, her voice is low, even, and careful. I know she has practiced this speech in her head, possibly in front of her mirror.

"Well, I just wanted to clarify where we are, how we stand, what's going on between us. I think we owe it to ourselves to be honest with each other."

This still isn't really a question, and I consider pointing that out to her. Instead, I sigh and shift slightly in my seat, rearranging my legs (my arthritic knees did not approve of our mall bonding time) as I continue to watch the sun flee.

"Are you even listening to me?" Her voice has a slight edge to it now, and stupidly, this pleases me because I want her to be off guard, I want her to be uncomfortable. It seems only fair.

"Yeah, I'm listening. I just don't know what you want me to say." I am being petulant, and I know it.

It's her turn to sigh, and I feel more than see her pull away from me. She puts her hands on the steering wheel and curls her fingers in, then out, then in again. I do the same thing when I am fighting to stay calm. I suddenly want to smile.

I look at her in profile, and in the fading sunlight, I am struck again by how beautiful she can be when she isn't trying. Dressed in jeans, in a sweatshirt, in tennis shoes, she has a sort of regal charm that she would never accept or believe. She looks nothing like the woman they cheer and clap for and pay obscene amounts of money to watch. I wonder if any of her fans would even recognize her in her street clothes—if one could call them fans. The smile, never fully formed, falls silently away.

"I guess …" She pauses. This is the moment where she will actually say something, and I know it is hard for her, but I need to hear it as much as she needs to actually say it. "I guess I just want to know if you want to be here. With me, with who I am, knowing me now, knowing me."

She closes her eyes when she says this last bit, it cost her something to be this vulnerable. It is my turn to gaze at her, and I wait until she opens her eyes and turns back toward me before I answer. It's my turn to say things that are difficult, and I won't shirk from this even if it hurts.

"Yes. Yes, I do. That's why I'm still here even though …" I know I can't address it head on; it is hard enough to even think about, so I shift gears. "I'm glad I'm getting a chance to know you."

Her eyes fill with tears, and I look away knowing that my eyes will do the same thing. Was it too much? Maybe I should have said less.

"Okay." Her voice is soft, the little girl voice from a lifetime ago. I haven't heard her little girl voice since she was five. "I'll be back to get you." I had lied, and she had looked at me and said "Okay." I wonder if she remembers.

The thought of that lie still haunts me, and I plunge on, not wanting to but unable to stop, "I'm not going to lie. I hate what you do for a living. It hurts and disgusts me that you …" I can't finish, the word *burlesque* seems too thick for my tongue, and I feel my cheeks warm. I didn't want that sort of life for her. Wasn't that the whole point? Closed adoption: saving her from living paycheck to paycheck with an alcoholic waitress of a mother in a dingy one-bedroom apartment and giving her a good family and a nice house in some suburb. They seemed like good Christian people. I had done the right thing. Everyone had said so.

It wasn't until I had been sober for a good four years that I had started to wonder, but even then, I had believed that the sacrifice was necessary, that she was better off. Eighteen years and seven months later, here we are sitting in a car that she owns outright, the backseat full of colorful shopping bags from dozens of stores. Inside them were hundreds of dollars worth of clothes that she had paid for without a blink of hesitation. She has an apartment in Milpitas, a college education, the support system of her adopted family, and a job that makes me nauseous to think about.

I close my eyes for a moment—mental intake of breath. I can hear her begin to speak, and I force myself to talk over her, to say the things that every daughter needs to hear from her mother even if they aren't true.

"But it doesn't matter; it doesn't matter. I love you anyway, and I'm proud of you. I wish I had been there for you. I wish things were different, but it doesn't matter because I'm here now, and it doesn't matter. It doesn't matter...."

We are both crying now, turned away from each other but sharing the same tears. The traffic is forgotten, the sunlight, the dinner reservation ... all of it is gone because after three lunch dates, countless circles walked in the mall, two manicures, and even the awkward moment in downtown with the flower vendor who thought we were partners, at last I am saying what she needs me to say, what she needs to believe. I tell myself it will be true someday. Maybe it already is a little.

The sun is gone now, hidden away behind the "Happy Italian Food," and the cars whizzing by throw their lights in at us. I am glad for the shadows. After a few moments of sniffing, she turns off the hazard lights and undoes the brake.

A moment later we are back with the traffic speeding our way down the street just like everyone else, adrift and yet swept along by the same current. She turns the radio back on, and even though her taste is music is atrocious, all loud bass lines and screaming clichés, I am grateful for the sound and the buffer that it gives.

Night Scape

I am standing in my living room listening to the quiet. There is no wind tonight, no cars hurrying by, and no animal noises even though the windows are open. It is late, or early, depending on how you look at it, and I have paused in my pacing to listen to the complete silence of the world.

I am not sleeping tonight. It isn't a matter of not wanting to because I know that it is good for me, that I need it, and that tomorrow (later today) is going to be rough. It isn't even that I can't sleep. If I were to take a few of my little white pills, I am sure I would be able to drift off rather quickly. I have had to turn to them in the past, and I don't feel any shame. But tonight I am not interested in sleeping.

My insomnia, if we must have a word to make it seem nonthreatening, has struck before. With almost fearful increasing speed, the days of perpetual fog are happening again. It is easy for me to accept that I won't sleep tonight. It isn't so easy to explain it to others.

If overly pressed to provide an explanation, I will say that there are two reasons I don't sleep—one or the other. Either internal or external. Externally, when the weather changes suddenly from warm to cold or surprises us with a freak thunder and lightning storm, I don't sleep because my nerves are suddenly on edge. I watch the rain, wondering what this sudden downpour symbolizes in my life. The wind holds secrets, and I listen to it screaming against the trees and over the rooftops. Of course, there are also the internal reasons I do not sleep. It is an artist's prerogative to be eccentric, and I have long reveled in my own uniqueness, my own art voice that would drive me from my bed and force me to create in the wee hours of the night. I used to say quite proudly that I did my best work at night. Other artists might prefer good natural light by which to paint, but I prefer darkness and solitude.

Things are different tonight as they have been for a long time—too long. My workroom is the one room that I can't quite bring myself to wander through. Again tonight, I float aimlessly past all the house's doors and windows and don't see them. I try to tell myself that tonight isn't about art; it's about something external. But my senses know better. The weather hasn't changed in weeks.

Perhaps it is because there hasn't been a change in the weather to blame, no real change in my life either—everything is how it has been for months, years even, and while it isn't particularly good, there is nothing in my life that is particularly bad either. The days stretch ahead with the slight mundane tone that one expects when things are just trucking along. It has been months since there has been anything worth getting excited about. I wander through the rooms of my home and try to remind myself why it is good to live a life without drama or strife.

We don't have conflict because we don't talk. By tacit agreement, we live our own lives, and while this situation isn't by any means ideal, it isn't horrible either. Any unhappiness I have can be blamed on my own desire for more. It isn't his fault that I am unhappy just as it isn't my fault that I no longer stimulate him intellectually or physically. Things happen, people grow older and change, time goes by....

He has retreated into his world of words, hiding himself in his study, even sometimes sleeping on his worn leather sofa. He emerges occasionally for coffee or booze, muttering to himself as he scans the newspaper, and then the door clicks shut, and the house falls silent again. Sometimes I pause outside the door and listen to the rustling of the pages. I strain my ears to hear his pen scratching against the paper and try to remember when the idea of him creating made me light-headed with pride.

At some point it became a competition. Then it became nothing at all. We gave up on sharing our work years ago—not because of a sudden calamity of spirit or malicious disregard for each other but simply because there was a part of me that doubted he would ever be able to create anything new, and in his eyes I saw the same thought reflected.

At this point I don't know if he would recognize me or I him. The artistic hippy flower child he married has moved on, and he is left with an ageing housewife who insists upon enjoying her insomnia. I sometimes wonder if he ever wakes in the middle of the night, if he too ever has the urge to pace, to move, to fight the walls of time and space. But, no, the scotch sees to that. He spends his nights in a stupor followed by the deep snoring sleep of a man past his prime. A man for whom there will always be a bottle nearby and no reason not to finish it. As always, thoughts of him make my already restless spirit twinge with the bitter mockery of age and passed chances. I admit defeat and move at last into my workroom.

It is mine. In true Virginia Woolf style no one else comes here, not him, not the cleaning girl, not even the various art students who show up asking for help or inspiration. They are fickle little children who still see me not as I am but as the tiny black-and-white picture of the still-aware (and virgin) version of myself that my agent likes to distribute as a sort of false advertising game of "Remember when …" This room was part of the reason that we bought the house in this already declining part of uptown. I had fallen in love with it on the first walk-through—its high ceiling and odd shape. It is long and narrow, and the door leading into the rest of the house is mirrored by the large bay window facing the sloping lawn to the east.

This is my own space, and I keep it organized and tidy, even if I was labeled Southland's "artist of casual chaos" a lifetime ago. The unused wood is stacked neatly; the jars are clean with none of the haphazard paint mess so popular by "expressionist" painters. The sheets of paper and pastels clutter the workbench but in a systematic way. This was a place for creativity but also a place where work was to be done, and I always secretly reveled in the idea of order.

Years ago I hung thick, heavy, dark red curtains over the window to block out all the outside light, rendering this room eternally night, eternally dark, eternally trapped in its own space and time. I had wanted a place where time would stop, where the daily routines and schedules could be forgotten. There would be no time-measuring devices in this sanctuary, I had declared. When I was working, I would be lost in the work itself, totally immune to the passage of time.

I had decorated with an eclectic eye to keep it timeless. In the center of the space hangs a wrought iron chandelier with sconces for candles glued in where the lightbulbs used to be. I did the makeover myself. What was once a shiny bobbleheaded dining room light is now a rickety and dangerous candle holder that swings precariously when I light the twenty-two mismatched candles.

Around the room there are tall, iron phallic-shaped candle holders bought from garage sales that compete loudly with the more quiet small brass wall sconces purchased at ridiculous prices from catalogues. Over the years I have added them how and when the mood struck, affixing them at crooked angles in any place I decided needed more light. Tonight, as in many nights recently, the feeling of timelessness has been more of a mockery than a comfort because nothing changes in this room except me.

I let my fingers run slowly over the jars of paint. Maybe there is inspiration to be found inside. Across the room in gloomy silence lie the pieces of blank wood awaiting use. The raw materials for my next project look just like the wood I used with the last project and the one before that. The recent finished products also tend to look alike in color, feel, and lack of being "new." Like the artistic expressions that came before them and the ones to follow, all of what I have created in the past five years comes out already feeling staged, old, and jaded. There is nothing new or bright in my color palates, and honestly, the piece I finished last summer that's leaning against the window in the kitchen could be swapped out for the framed piece upstairs on the landing that was done three summers ago. No one would notice.

The most recent piece of wood has an imperfection that I found compelling months ago, but now the flaw in the grain seems to be nothing more than a reflection of myself. Useless and unnatural, not part of anything good, and completely interchangeable with any of the other artistic expressions found on gallery walls or in biographical books. The notch in the wood seemed to point out the obvious fact that I paint in the wee hours of the morning because I can't think of anything else to do. A lot of the time I paint because he expects me to. He did, after all, marry an artist. He grows old with his manuscripts, and I retreat into my workroom to be creative and earn the reputation of a working artist so that we can all continue to ignore the fact that any talent I might have had at one point is not being encouraged or cultivated here. I have been painting out of habit for years. Now, even that habit has fled, and I can't paint at all.

I line up the bottles of paint on the workbench behind a row of pure white sphere candles and lift the new piece of wood up to rest behind them, hoping that the shadow reflections of the colors will inspire me. I light all seven candles, systematically snuff them out one at a time, and then relight them. Perhaps a new spark might create a new shadow. The open window lets in a faint breeze, and I wish desperately for a bird song, a tree rustle, something to remind me that there is more than me and the silent wind alive on this dark night.

* * *

Another night when sleep won't come naturally. Another night where I stood for long moments looking down at the pills in my hand before letting them fall one by one into the toilet bowl and be flushed away. I looked at myself in the mirror and felt a faint sense of revulsion.

Tonight I wore white, a long silk nightgown that was just the sort of thing he used to admire, and I touched him softly, carefully, with gentle kisses on his collarbone, just the way I used to do when we were young, ardent lovers necking in my father's car. It was a long shot, to try to entice him away from the comfort of his study, but tonight, instead of turning away or brusquely brushing me off like an errant wisp of hair, he had closed his book and followed me up the stairs, his hands clutching the banister, and his breathing already heavy.

I had left the nightstand light on and faced him in the semidarkness. Turning away from me, he undressed, his movements slow and calculating, and I was shocked (as I always am when I bother to notice) by his stooped shoulders, his gray hair, and the parts of him that sag. I had forced myself to stay still, to not look away, and when he turned to face me at last, wearing nothing but his old man's underpants, I was ready. Instead of sliding next to him and letting him undress me under the blankets, I held his eyes with mine and began to untie the straps of my gown. First one side, then the other, and I let the top fall forward, my breasts bare.

He made a move to stop me, but I continued, slowly and deliberately watching myself in the mirror over the vanity as I shed the sheer white fabric until I stood before him completely exposed. My reflection self moved her hands over her body carefully, first one breast and then the other, past the scar across the abdomen, over the skin so thin, the veins so dark. My eyes filled with tears, and I turned away to find him watching me, a look on his face that said more than he had articulated in years. He reached out and took my hand in his and brought it to his soft weak lips, but I pulled away before the moment of contact and turned off the light.

Later, against the sounds of his snores, I shut the bedroom door with a feeling of quiet escape. His advances in the dark had been predictable and though sweet and well practiced (we have been lovers on and off for more than twenty-seven years now) had done little to bring himself to a state of readiness, and eventually he had rolled off of me. A moment later I heard the sound of the unnoticed nightstand bottle being opened. He had gulped the Scotch and then had lain back. Moments later his breath was deep and rhythmic, and he hadn't stirred when I sought refuge in the bathroom.

Facing myself in the mirror was almost impossible, but I forced myself to look unblinking into my own eyes and hold the gaze of the crone reflection until tears made it too blurry to see and I gave up, wrapping myself in a worn bathrobe and fleeing.

Downstairs I move haltingly over the carpet, my feet barely leaving the ground. I decide not to turn on any lights tonight. The darkness will be my companion, my secret voyeur. I shed my robe as I pass by the couch, the entertainment unit, the framed pictures of family and friends and enter the workroom, bare and open for inspiration. I light every single candle and burn sweet, smoky incense.

In the flickering light I watch my shadow dance in time with the curling wisps of smoke. I lift my arms up high and sway my head from side to side letting my hair flow around my shoulders and back. In my mind I am an exotic fire dancer, part shampoo commercial, part wild woman of the night full of unbridled sexual appetites. I drink a bottle of cheap red wine as quickly as possible and lie down with my body pressed against the blank wooden panels. I close my eyes, and though I won't sleep, I concentrate on dreaming against the empty places.

* * *

Tonight I don't even consider the pills. The quickness in my blood told me hours ago that there would be no sleep. I consider the pacing, the waiting, the quiet firelight and self-loathing. Systematically I reject these things. Tonight I will seek inspiration from the outside, the external. In the master bathroom, I watch myself through the mirror. All in red, my body is held tight in clothes that leave little to the imagination. I have painted red and orange flames on my shoulders and my upper thighs. I leave a blood-colored lipstick signature on the counter next to my bottle of white pills and move with determined steps down the stairs. I pause in the doorway of my workroom and consider briefly stepping inside for a last look at the blank wood, but I can't handle the silent contempt with which it holds me, and my bravado might not last. I leave the house.

Moments tick by, and who can say how long it is until I find myself in a crowded dance club, my body pressed upon by the other patrons, my skin alive and slightly damp. I turn this way and that, pushing through the crowd as if I have a destination. In the center of the dancing, I fit myself between the others and close my eyes. I am nothing but a drop of water in transition. My body moves to the beat, and my head lolls from side to side in supreme surrender. I bend and touch the floor with my whole hand feeling the beat of the music echoing up from somewhere more primal than the earth.

There is a man with his hands on my hips. He steadies me, and I let myself slip so that his groping will have purpose, even if only imagined. He grinds himself against my back and breathes hotly against my neck. The lights spin, and the crowd is frantic with movement, but in this moment, all my senses are fixated on the stranger whose tongue is making lazy circles on the nape of my neck in direct contradiction to the hurried beat of the music. Here is a soul who is delighting in the slowness even while we are drowning in a sea of speed and ecstasy. It is the juxtaposition that intrigues me more than anything else. I turn myself around in his arms and let him continue his exploration of my skin with his mouth.

We move to the bar, to the patio, to the dance floor, to the sidewalk … the phases of this tryst are as important as the tryst itself. The buildup is fascinating as he goes from ardent seducer to nervous boy-child in my arms and back again to dream lover, his body smooth and pulled taught with the tension that only letting go can release. I won't let him speak. There is no need to hear his voice; it is enough to hear his breathing. How can I tell him that I live in silence, and his words will not make a difference? I trace my hands over his back, pulling him in and then pushing him away in a mock coital dance that enamors him even if he doesn't know why.

We go to another club—the music is the same, the people are still drunk, and the lights still flash like chaos itself transcended into a plaything for the masses. In the blinking and sputtering white-hot spotlights, we find our peace. Together as one we sway to the music, and now his hands are insistent and yearning; my skirt is lifted in time with the music, and he presses himself against me with just the faintest ounce of urgency.

I watch myself in the spinning disco ball of light. The wild woman, aged huntress of the tribe, midwife to other people's passions, hair free and swinging, body tight and supple at the same time, moving with newfound grace to the sounds of youth and frustration. She gives into his voiceless passion, and she is beautiful, a creature of the divine in his eyes and mine. But in the moment of release, she becomes nothing more than a mockery of something more grotesque and barbaric. Her eyes are glazed; the fire on her skin is smeared, and there is a definite tremble in her movements. There are tangles in her hair and a run in her stocking; sweat has made her chest and stomach wet; and her breath reeks of eventual death. She pulls away from her illusions, pushing against the dancers who want to keep her and weaving her way through the lights to find peace outside and alone, where with huge gulping breaths, I become myself again in the dark.

It isn't hard to find a cab or to give directions. These things happen from some kind of instinct, just like treading softly on the stairs in a quiet home. The cab driver knows enough to not ask, and I huddle in the backseat, gently touching the bruises on my thighs and hips with wondering fingers. At the driveway, I press money into his hand and watch as the taillights, two red judgmental eyes, fade down the quiet street. I can't quite bring myself to go inside, so I sit in a small heap on the lawn, my shoes discarded somewhere near the flowerbed. One of the neighbor's lawns erupts in a crescendo of sprinkler water, and I start to shiver.

I return to my workroom, my body sticky and sore, tired and dazed. I open the window, push aside the heavy curtains, and let the night light in. Dawn is on its way. It is only a matter of moments until the birds start singing. They are the truth that the night denies in its barrenness. Almost as an afterthought I remove the visages of my night's adventure and drop the whole mess—dress, stockings, soiled panties—into a testimonial pile and push it aside. I face the window stripped of my disguise and feel the breeze against my skin. With fresh paint I mark out the smeared flames with cool blue teardrops. There is no need to light candles tonight, because I am no longer afraid of the dark.

I lay the scarred piece of wood across my legs with no regard for the splinters that it threatens, dip my fingers into the freshly opened bottles, and paint as the sun comes up.

Coffee Date

We meet under the marquee downtown, 6:00 PM on the dot. I have been waiting in the Starbucks across the street for an hour, watching the time with occasional furtive glances at my cell phone while trying to look busy and unapproachable. Every seven and a half minutes a train pulls into the station across the street, and I watch through the smudgy window next to my table as throngs of people frantically fight each other to get through the automatic doors. There is no order, no "stay to the right, and we can all board and disembark in an orderly fashion," just a mass of cold, hurried people intent on themselves. I envy them in their driven, single-minded purpose.

At 5:58 I collect my notebook, my pens (three, just in case), my almost empty coffee cup, and my purse. I wrap my scarf around my neck, feeling instantly safer, and push my way through the people waiting in line. Outside the air is crisp and cold, but the sky above is clear as I walk over to the front of the theater, trying to ignore the pounding of my heart.

I glance at my phone. Then, almost without realizing it, I look up, and there he is. He's walking toward me from Pitching Street, baseball hat shadowing his face, hands thrust into the pockets of an unfamiliar coat, dodging around college kids and a group of loud boisterous men who have just emerged energized and glowing from the gym. I watch him casually sidestep a woman talking on her cell phone as she runs by oblivious to the world (and giving the whole street and her unfortunate listener the frantic play-by-play) as she tries to catch the train. Our eyes meet, and he smiles.

I look down, suddenly shy, and busy myself with unplugging my iPod, wrapping up the cord, fiddling with the zipper of my purse, tightening my scarf until he is standing right in front of me and I can't put it off any longer. I paste a smile on my face and look up.

Because of the lights, because of the darkness, I can't really see his eyes, and I am glad because I hope this means he can't see mine either. It's bad enough that he can see the rest of me.

He is smiling still, and he says my name and moves forward. Suddenly we are hugging, and I try to say his name, but I can't, partly because my mouth is full of scarf and partly because it would hurt too much. The hug is sweet, short, and leaves me disoriented. He pulls away and laughs at my mouth full of scarf and then steps back and looks me up and down.

"You look good."

I am reeling from his physical nearness and almost gasping from the emotional distance. Mainly, I am horribly disappointed in myself for losing any self-repose I might have had in Starbucks. I blush from the compliment, knowing it is false, and return the truthful favor.

"Thanks. You too!"

He pushes his hands into his pockets and leans back, still looking me up and down. I move my purse to the other arm and decide to take control.

"So, you hungry? Wanna grab some dinner … or …"

"Nah, I had a big lunch." There is a beat; the ball is in his court, and he knows it. After all, it was him who made contact; this whole thing is because of him. It always was. I wait.

"Let's just grab a drink and walk around. Is that cool? Feel like a cup of coffee?"

I swig the final dregs of my mocha and toss the cup in the nearby trashcan.

"Sure!"

And just like that the tension is gone, and I don't care why he called or what we may or may not discuss or why he waited eight years to call in the first place. We laugh because if there is one thing that stays constant, it's my addiction to coffee. He echoes my thoughts as we walk back over to Starbucks.

"Should have known you would be up for coffee. Never heard you turn it down before."

"Some things don't change," I say, letting my mind skip hurriedly over the things—the many, many things—that do. "That's me, coffee junkie."

He remembers what I always order, and we stand close because the shop is crowded. I am sweating in my coat, but my hands are still cold. I twist the place where my ring used to be and feel his eyes on me, but when I look up, he is studying the rows of cookies and muffins with intense concentration. Ordering small talk ensues; I realize that the barista probably thinks we are just another couple out on just another date if she even bothers to spare a thought for us at all. I let him pay.

We walk in silence with the occasional sip of coffee as the early holiday crowds press around us. In the park they are setting up for what will be Christmas In The Park in just a matter of days. They used to wait until after Thanksgiving, but now early November sees the carting out of large wooden trains, sparkling lights, and piped in holiday music. Soon, it will be magical and bright; right now, it is containers still closed, trailers parked randomly, and a few errant stakes in the grass marking the spots for community Christmas trees and the location for the stage.

We sit on one of the benches, close enough to touch but not touching, and survey the scene. People watching was always something we did well together, and without thought, we slip right back into the familiar pattern.

"That lady over there," he leans in, his breath warm on my ear, "she works for the Fairmont, runs the seventeenth floor."

"What happens on the seventeenth floor?" I ask, watching the woman in an unfortunate red dress and gold heels as she hurries through the crowd.

"Everything … and nothing," he answers. "It's like Vegas. Things go on up there, silly, crazy, circus-type stuff, but they drug you so that you don't really remember it. Clients leave with a vague sense that they had a great time, but because they can't totally remember, they have to come back again and again."

"So, what really happens on the seventeenth floor?" I ask again, knowing my part in the exchange, knowing that the next story to spin will be on my shoulders. I glance around the park already picking out my victim and only loosely paying attention as he continues.

"Well, first they brainwash you, then they make you into zombies.… Afterward, there's tap dancing.…"

We exchange absurd stories about the people in the park until the crowd thins and the wind picks up, bringing with it the scent of rain approaching. My coffee is long gone, and I shiver. We have fallen silent, and the awkwardness is back, lying itself on my shoulders and wrapping itself around my chest.

"So …" He breaks the silence, and I jump up.

"I need more coffee." Looking everywhere but at him, I sling my purse back over my shoulder. "It's colder now, and if we're going to talk, I need more coffee."

He hesitates, frustration clouding his features, but I am standing firm. Finally, he forces a smile that doesn't quite reach his eyes. "Okay, you're the boss. More coffee it is."

I turn and walk away, knowing he will follow, knowing I need this space, knowing I am a coward. The silence isn't comfortable as we leave the park, and instinctively I turn toward Saint Michael's and head to the Starbucks off of Sixth. I need the distraction of lights, of the crowded streets that are starting to fill up with the noisy bar crowd now that the noisy shopping crowd is safely home. I need the press of strangers against my body, I need …

I need to snap out of it. I realize I am walking fast, too fast, and that he probably can tell that I'm upset. (He always could.) I breathe through my nose and try to calm myself down. Why am I mad at him already? He hasn't even said whatever it is that he felt the need to say, I rationalize while I try to slow my pace and then work on displacing my anger (years of therapy finally coming in handy). He hasn't done anything (yet) to warrant me acting, or walking, like a bitch. I slow my steps even more, and within moments we are once again strolling side by side down the street, the picture of a happy couple on a coffee date.

I know why I am upset, and the realization makes me blush. I had really hoped that things would have gone differently. Standing in front of my mirror, I had envisioned our greeting with all the heart-fluttering action and soundtrack magic of every romantic comedy. He would gaze deeply into my eyes and then reach out and tuck a charmingly errant lock of hair behind my ear. His hand would linger, and then he would place his palm against my cheek and rub his thumb gently across my cheekbone. Unable to control himself, he would kiss me … gently at first but soon with growing passion until we were the subject of stares and catcalls but utterly lost in the rapture of being together.

Obviously, that hadn't happened.

We enter the Starbucks and join the line of fellow addicts. I had forgotten that this Starbucks was habitually slower than any other Starbucks in the Midtown area, and I think briefly about giving up or going somewhere else, but a quick glance back at him, and I decide to stay where I am. Whatever he has come to tell me can wait another twenty minutes.

The text message had been brief, out of the blue, and totally to the point: "It's Sam. I need to see you. Can you meet me tomorrow night?" I hadn't heard my phone go off because it had fallen behind the couch, and so I got his message three hours after it had been delivered to my inbox. For what seemed like an eternity, I sat on the floor, half behind the couch myself, and simply looked at my phone. Inwardly, the struggle between joy and despair had started, and that particular battle had yet to be resolved. I had shut the phone with a soft click and set it on top of the entertainment center next to Clair's movies and homemade popsicle-stick figures with yarn hair. For the next twenty minutes I sat at the dining room table still strewn with the breakfast dishes and the remnants of her most recent art project (something involving crayons and empty egg cartons; she refused to tell me what it was, admonishing me in her high-pitched seven-year-old voice to be patient) and had thought.

The first question was whether to admit that it was still my number and that he had actually reached me. The next thing was to figure out what he knew. Or did he know anything at all? The only way to know for sure would be to respond.

Hands shaking, I had responded with a simple yes. The time and location had come zipping back at me moments later. There had been no other communication, but there had been times in the last twenty hours when I had wondered if this was perhaps an elaborate hoax on the part of some evil person or some cruel twist of circumstance. My number hadn't changed, but how had he known? Had he simply sent the message out like a cry in the dark hoping it would find its way to me and not some other person? Why hadn't he just called? But then I thought of answering the phone in the midst of helping Clair brush her teeth or stirring something on the stove and knew that I wouldn't have been able to function if his voice had suddenly sounded in my ear.

People have had heart attacks with less provocation, and the slamming shock and near paralysis of reading the text had been dramatic enough.

I had sleepwalked through the rest of the evening and had spent all of last night lying on my bed with the covers pulled up tight, staring at the ceiling and listening to the clock in the living room count down the seconds. All throughout the day I had swung back and forth like a rusty pendulum between thrilled excitement and absolute dread. Half the time I had railed against the idea of (still) being at his beck and call. But morbid curiosity and the vague hope that with a touch, with a kiss, with a single magic word, he could make it all better had plagued my thoughts as well. Standing in the kitchen this afternoon and looking at the mess only a second grader can make, I knew that I had to come, if only to reassure myself.

I had practiced my speech almost nonstop on the drive to Midtown, and I had even written part of it out in the parking garage before walking to Starbucks and settling in for the wait. My words, full of poise and certainty, seemed to burn from the inside of my purse, mocking me.

"Too much time has gone by…. It wouldn't be fair to either one of us…. There is so much I wanted to tell you…. I did you a favor in coming here tonight, but I can't see you…. You have to accept that I've moved on…. I'm so sorry…."

I would have been firm and gentle; I would have held his hand softly and looked pointedly away when he got emotional. I would have been strong. I would find closure. After the kissing, of course.

Instead, I buy us a round of coffee and lead the way back outside. We stand on the corner not really going left or right; I am suddenly at a loss. The coffee was my final buffer, and I am unsure of where to go.

"Come on," he says, taking a decisive sip. "This way." I follow, feeling somehow chastised.

Three blocks later he stops at Saint Michael's and climbs the steps. We sit at the top near one of the columns and look out over Michael's Square. The city has put decorations up in the trees, and the whole square is bathed in fuzzy white light. From here we can see most of what used to be the historical part of Midtown before the flood. A flash of memory, and I am seeing an old newspaper picture of flood survivors huddled on these very steps begging for help from the church. I try, but I can't remember if the church had helped. I'm sure it had, but at the same time I have a feeling that its inability to provide succor to the displaced of the city had been the point of the newspaper article to begin with.

He puts down his cup of coffee and turns toward me. I brace myself and look at him. There is still a tiny part of me that wants him to hold me, to kiss me, to beg me to take him back. A much larger part of me just wants him to say whatever it is so that I can go home. I am suddenly very tired, and I don't care why he is here.

I don't care.

I really ... don't care. I think my mouth drops open in surprise because I see him hesitate. He is about to speak, but I beat him to it.

"I don't care."

He blinks at me. I let out a breath I hadn't known I was holding and plunge on, finding strength as the words flow.

"*I don't care*. I know you're here to tell me something, and I know it isn't what I thought I wanted to hear, but I just now, just now, realized that I don't care. You want to say something, something that will change our lives or at least make some sort of impact. Otherwise, what would be the point, right? And I just ... I just don't care." Giggles are threatening, and I take a big gulp of coffee. He opens his mouth to speak, but I rush on. "No, really. It's been eight years, *eight years* without a sound, without anything, and I always thought I needed something from you, and just now I realized that I *don't.*"

I smile at him and see an uneasy smile in return. He doesn't believe me, but that's okay. I believe myself.

"But I really feel like ..." I put my fingers on his lips, feel the slight thrill of contact and feel it fade almost as quickly as it came. Somehow I find the ability to be gentle even now.

"I know. But I think there are things better left unsaid. *Unknown.*"

He takes that in and then looks away over the square below us. We sit, not touching, not talking, and I lean back on the steps, relaxed and unhurried. In a moment I know I will get up and walk back to the parking garage and drive home. If I hurry, I can be there in time to read the bedtime story and supervise the teeth brushing. I know I will drive quickly without the distraction of the radio and that I won't look back. I know he won't follow me; we both know it's over.

The sound of the traffic carries to us as the wind picks up again, reminding me that soon there will be rain, and there will be a lot of it.

The Unnamed Princess

When Julie was in third grade, she wrote a short story. This was not the only story she would write; Julie was certain of this fact, but it was her first, and she was proud of it. She carefully tore out three lined pages from her notebook and wrote her story in big block letters. She left space between each paragraph for a picture.

The story was very simple because Julie liked simple stories that were easy to remember and tell again later. In her story there was a beautiful princess who had escaped from an evil fairy but then got lost in a dark and scary forest. The princess wandered around the forest for days looking for helpful talking animals, but all the animals were mean and looked like they would rather eat the princess than talk to her. They didn't eat her, however, because Julie felt that having the princess die in this manner would be counterproductive to the "happily ever after" ending she was going for. Eventually, the princess found her way home and was joyfully greeted by her parents. The three of them did indeed live happily ever after. No one knows what happened to the evil fairy. Julie herself had completely forgotten all about her by the time she was vividly describing the happy homecoming scene.

The story itself did not cause even a ripple in the lives of her classmates, whom Julie hid from at recess in order to write in secret, but it did cause some ripples at home. After reading her story to her family that night at dinner (meat loaf and mashed potatoes—it was Wednesday), Julie announced she was going to be a writer when she grew up. Her little sister Henrietta (younger than Julie by two years and thus completely enthralled by the story) clapped excitedly. Julie's parents were excited by neither the story nor the announcement.

"You should be a mother, instead," said Julie's mother who had never wanted to be anything but a mother and who felt it a sad state of affairs when young girls wanted to work outside the home.

"Maybe I'll be both," Julie retorted, sure that such a thing was possible even though being a mother held no thrall for her. Her mother rolled her eyes and went to get dessert.

"You should go into business instead," shouted her father. He always shouted, having lost part of his hearing in the war. Julie's family didn't take it personally. "Just today there was a guy who had gone into business in the shop. He didn't even look at the sales slip when it was time to pay. That's how much money he had."

Julie's father was a mechanic, and he always said you could tell how successful someone was by how they acted when they were given the bill for their car repairs. People always forgot how seldom they needed work done on their cars, and most people complained about how much it cost. No one complained about how much going to the doctor cost or how much bread cost, Julie's father would shout, so why should they complain about getting their car fixed? Julie, who was sure that people did in fact complain about how much bread and doctor appointments cost, had learned a long time ago to nod and smile at her father when he started on this old familiar rant. She did so now. "Never even glanced down," mumbled her father as he ate his dessert.

Julie and Henrietta, who had unfortunately been labeled Henri earlier that year in first grade and would bear the masculine nickname for the entirety of her short life, went outside to eat their desserts in the backyard. They sat on the grass with their bowls of ice cream, and Julie placed her story on the step behind them. She had heard about "dirty" stories, and she didn't want hers to be one of them—better to keep it up on the step during dessert. Ice cream tended to be messy, at least for Julie.

"Are you really going to be a writer?" asked Henri, who had left her spoon inside and was slurping with zeal.

"I don't know," Julie answered. "Maybe. When I get older and have something to write about. It would have to be something big and important." She ate slowly, licking her spoon completely clean before dipping it back into the melting ice cream.

"Well," Henri said, putting her empty bowl down on the grass and eyeing Julie's not empty bowl out of the corner of her eye, "I liked your story, even if it didn't have a name."

To Henri, everything needed to have a name. She was learning her letters and words, and it was important to her that things had names. If something had a name, she reasoned, it had a word. And when things had words, she could write them down. Henri thought it would be great fun to write the names of things all over the things themselves. She pictured herself running around with a big black marker naming the entire world. She could start with her mom, she often thought wistfully, and would write in really big letters MOM so that everyone would know. Other words she would write on her mother were OLD and TIRED and WOMAN. Julie's mother would probably not like having these things written on her, so it was good that Henri only thought about doing her big naming project occasionally and usually when she was outside. Inside the house, and thus closer to big black pens, Henri was easily distracted by other fun things to do, such as drop pennies in the radiator or reorganize the sheet music on the piano. Thus, Julie's mother never did get properly named.

Julie sat in the fading sunlight of the backyard and thought about what she should have named her story. Henri was right; it needed a name. Absently, she gave Henri the rest of her ice cream and lay back on the grass, looking up at the sky. Forgetting to name her story, to give it a title, made her feel stupid—like forgetting socks on a cold day or having two different-colored gloves. She was sure that real writers didn't ever forget to give their stories a title; they probably had the titles all picked out before they even started writing.

"It has a name," she lied to Henri, not wanting her little sister to know that she wasn't a real writer. "It's called 'The Princess in the Woods,' and it's going to have pictures and everything." She didn't know where these pictures would come from, but she had left space for them, so it seemed like just a matter of time before they would come along. She sat up and smiled triumphantly at her sister whose face and hands were sticky with ice cream and who had, in the manner of all six-year-olds, forgotten completely what the topic of conversation had been. Henri smiled back at her and then rolled her eyes when they heard the bath water start.

"Quick," Julie told her sister. "Hide!" A moment later, the back door opened, and Julie's mother stuck her head out. Julie picked up her story and did her best to look adult and innocent at the same time.

"Time for your baths. Where's your sister?" Julie's mother didn't ever call Henrietta by her full name, she preferred "her" and "your sister/daughter" or at times of extreme emotion "baby."

Julie shrugged and flipped the pages of her story slowly. A tiny suppressed giggle floated up from under the porch, and Julie made herself hiccup to distract her mother.

"Well go get her and tell her it's bath time." Julie's mother hadn't heard the giggle or the fake hiccup. She was busy listening to the bath water and worrying that it was going to overflow. Julie's mother was the kind of woman who worried about everything she couldn't see.

"I don't know where she is. She disappeared." Julie kept her eyes away from her mother as she talked.

"Well it isn't as if she simply vanished. She had to have gone somewhere. Stop playing and go get her." Julie's mother went back inside to check the bath water and flicked on the porch light. She called back over her shoulder, "Hurry up, the water will get cold." For Julie's mother, bath time was a very serious matter.

Well, Julie thought to herself, she *could* have vanished. What if it was haunted under the porch? What if some other little girl had climbed under there a long time ago to get out of having to take a bath and gotten stuck? What if her family had gone on vacation and had forgotten her, and she had died and was angry? What if she had been waiting all this time for some other little girl to sneak under the porch so she could grab her and squeeze her and not let her go? Julie leaped off the porch and lay down on the ground peering into the shadows for Henri. The porch light made the backyard brighter, but it seemed to make under the porch even darker.

"Henri? Are you there?" *Relax,* Julie told herself, *you heard her giggle just a second ago ...* but then her imagination went racing off again like a drunken bee. What if that hadn't been a giggle? What if that had been the last bit of air escaping from poor Henri's lungs as the ghost girl squeezed her to death under the very porch where Julie had been sitting? Julie shut her eyes, sure that her little sister was dead under there in the dark and that it was all her fault. She felt dizzy and weak; visions of the ghost girl, nothing more than a black skeleton with oozy green skin and spiderweb pigtails, swam before her eyes.

Suppose, Julie thought wildly, that the ghost girl knew it was Julie who had sent Henri under the porch ... suppose the ghost girl was still lonely because Henri had a tendency to clam up when she was nervous, and Julie was sure that being grabbed by a ghost girl would have made Henri very nervous. Was she next? Was the ghost girl planning even now on grabbing her and dragging her under the porch to join her dead sister? Julie knew she should open her eyes and look, but she was too terrified to move.

A small, dirty hand suddenly touched Julie's shoulder. She gagged on her own scream and threw herself away from the porch. Franticly, she rolled back onto the grass and crouched, staring at the darkness. A second later she let out a huge breath as Henri pulled herself out from under the porch and sat blinking in the light.

Julie grabbed her sister and hugged her tight, elated that they had both survived. Henri, however, had not had the benefit of her sister's terror and was repulsed by the sudden affection.

"Ew," she told her sister who looked like she was about to cry. "It was dirty under there."

Reflection

June hung up the phone, and for a long moment, she contemplated picking it up off the desk and throwing it. The act of violence, so against the grain of her passive self, was tempting. She imagined the satisfying crunch of plastic as it hit the wall, the receiver springing free, and the thud as the whole thing hit the floor of her office.

Of course, the phone was plugged in with two cords (one slick gray and the other an unsightly yellow), and the idea of them aborting her attempt and simply ripping themselves out of their sockets, catching the phone midflight, and making it clatter to an unsatisfying halt far from the wall made her pause. There was also the idea that to give into such a base display of emotion would make her, in her own eyes at least, little more than a petulant child. If there was one thing that she wanted to see in herself, it was rock-steady control. With a sigh, she gave up the errant thought of aggression. She was better than that.

With a few decisive clicks, she shut down the programs on her computer and logged off. The familiar Windows Shutdown Coda (as Margie called it) sang out at her, strangely loud in the quiet room. She was the last to leave again today, and she was glad. Her co-workers were nice women, but the phone call had been horribly emotional and personal, and she was relieved that there hadn't been any witnesses. The fact that he had had the audacity to call her at work after all this time—knowing that she would be working late, knowing that she wouldn't be able to refuse to meet him—made her angry. But the thought of seeing him again after six months and eleven days (not that she was counting) filled her with decidedly more complicated feelings. The truth was she wanted to see him as much as she wanted to breathe, but she had always pictured their next meeting to be, first, at her request and, second, at a place and time of her choosing.

Any delusions of such a meeting had promptly flown out the window when she had answered her phone twenty minutes ago. She had been sure that it was Margie calling from her car with "just one more last-minute thing" for her to do before leaving work. Everyone knew that she worked late. Margie even knew why. "Oh, honey, you take all the time you need; you work as much as you need," was Margie's way of being both a boss and a friend.

"Accounts, this is June." She had answered the phone the same way she always did, quickly and without bothering to check the caller ID. If it wasn't Margie, it would be one of the lawyers. She had already grabbed a pencil and a yellow post-it, ready to take notes.

"It's David."

For a moment the room had spun crazily out of control. She had felt like a cartoon character that blinks in amazement when the ground underfoot suddenly becomes nothing.

"June, you there?"

He knew she was there, her fingers going white as she squeezed the phone, her eyes glazing over, her heart jumping into her throat.

"David?"

"Yeah, listen. I'm downstairs. I want to talk to you."

She had let out a breath she hadn't even known she was holding. *He wanted to talk. He wanted to talk. He* wanted *to* talk*?!*

From ancient memory came the voice of Lia, a mighty force in Women Who Won't Whimper, a militant feminist group at Clayton University that June had joined during her attempt at becoming a strong feminist. Despite giving her "all" for the cause with the marches, the rallies, the civil disobedience, and the loud and chaotic burning of bras and breaking of mirrors in the quad, she had somehow managed to get a degree in business. She had also ultimately given her "all" to a swimmer named Patrick and had been kicked out of W4 for not being enough of a radical. Patrick left her soon after that for much the same reason. She hadn't thought of Lia (or Patrick) in more than six years, but it was Lia's voice that she heard deep in her own when she answered him.

"I don't really think there's anything we need to talk about." It was a calm voice, an in-control type of voice, a voice that only hinted at the whirlwind of bitchiness that lay just under the surface. June had once seen Lia reduce a local journalist to tears in a conversation that had started in this same cold voice.

"Well, I do."

A tear threatened to fall. She blinked rapidly, trying to keep from shaking. "*Yes,*" she wanted to scream, "Let's talk…. Let's talk about it…. talk, talk, talk…." But, again, it was an echo of Lia's voice that came through, detached and a few degrees colder.

"No, David, I don't have time." And then, because she was still herself and because Lia had always scared her a little bit, she added in her own voice, "I'm sorry."

"Don't be a bitch, June. I can wait out here all night."

Ahhh, there was the David she remembered. The David with his own barely-under-the-surface anger.

As if reading her mind, he continued in a softer tone. "I just want to talk. Come on down. Let's deal with this like adults."

She waited, but Lia's influence had left as quickly as it had arrived. Alone, she didn't stand a chance. "Give me twenty minutes."

"Fine." He sounded like wanted to argue the point, but she hadn't given him the chance by carefully hanging up the phone.

The computer clicked off, and she stared at it with unfocused eyes. The emptiness of the screen still slightly unnerved her. She had grown up in a world of computers, but it was only in the last few years that the glass monitors with their sloping reflections and fuzzy static sounds had been replaced by the more practical but impersonal LCD screens. The sheer emptiness of them bothered her because they reminded her of just how detached everything was and because she still always expected to see herself looking back. There was always a moment of quiet panic when she glanced at a dark screen and saw nothing.

She blinked, coming back into the present. Why was she thinking about this now? Lia's voice made a booming comeback, the impatience a scalding refrain. "Because you're procrastinating."

With a sigh, she picked up her purse, clicked off the lights, and shut the outer door of the legal wing behind her. At the elevators she hesitated. *If I run to the bathroom, I can comb my hair, maybe fix my lipstick....* Lia's voice was firm. "Don't even think about it. You aren't going down there to impress him. Go down there, tell him to fuck off, and go home."

She pressed the elevator button and waited. In the metal doors she could see a vague reflection of herself, all colors and shapes with nothing overly defined. Her salmon sweater and black pants appeared horrendously enlarged, but her face was nothing more than a peach smudge under limp hair that seemed to be going for blond and had given up at ash. *There's no way I can go down there and see him like this,* she thought. *I need to at least see myself before I see him. I have to prepare.*

The elevator doors opened smoothly, parting her reflection down the middle. She envisioned herself getting into the car, turning, pushing the lobby button, and watching the little red numbers countdow ... but she watched this as her feet, on their own accord, ignored the phantom Lia and stomped down the carpeted hall and into the ladies' room.

In the mirror she glared at another unfocused reflection. Now it was her face that was blurry and enlarged. She ran cold water and watched it fall in a steady stream from the faucet into the dark, inviting hole. Leaning over, she strained her eyes to see deeper into the sink even as Lia's voice continued to mock her lack of a backbone.

Mesmerized by the water, she concentrated on her breathing and let herself lose track of time, her head down, hair falling around her shoulders, eyes only partly open. It seemed a long time ago that the phone had rung. Surely it hadn't actually happened. It was just a daydream, like the time she thought she had fallen asleep at her desk and spent the night in the building. Well, no, not exactly like that. She had fallen asleep at her desk, but instead of wandering the empty building as a ghost version of herself all night, she had only drifted off for about twenty minutes before a phone call from Stan in purchasing awoke her. She remembered how befuddled she had felt for the rest of the day, sure that she had lived through a long and horribly lonely night as a waiflike apparition with no reflection … sure that it was already Thursday … some part of her not trusting the date and time display on her computer screen.

This was nothing like that, she assured herself. The phone call had happened, and she was very much her large salmon-sweatered self standing in this restroom putting off seeing the man who she had spent a good five years being madly in love with and the past six months being furious at.

The thing was she didn't want to go down there, and it had nothing to do with the fact that she was afraid and everything to do with the fact that she could anticipate exactly how it would go.

She would get off the elevator, and he would be leaning against his car in front of the main doors, directly across from her. He would stand perfectly still as she walked through the lobby, her heels clicking uncomfortably loud on the tiles, and would watch her fumble in her purse for her security badge so that she could open the main door without setting off the alarm.

She didn't know what sort of greeting she should offer—after all, it was he who had left her, he who had disappeared down the hospital hallway, he who had not bothered to answer his phone. She had been the one to do all the talking, to do all the explaining, to drive herself home. (He had been nice enough to leave the keys on the bedside table.)

She thought quickly about that homecoming—her body still bruised, her mind still a torment of anger and blame. She had parked in the garage and gone inside by the side door, ready to do battle, ready to scream at him, to throw it in his face. Ready also to listen to his excuses, ready (in her heart, she knew) to accept whatever sort of apology he chose to give her, ready to take him back and play the part of the martyr. Ready to continue in the life they had built together.

Had she felt shame in those moments when she was so sure of what was about to happen? She didn't think so; shame had come later with shock as she walked though the mostly empty house and realized that he had left her. He had gone home while she lay in the ICU barely breathing and telling lies to the cops, and he had packed up his stuff and disappeared. Until tonight.

Would he try to hug her hello? Would she let him?

She let her mind skip over the greeting. She wanted to plan out her words because she was just so very confused. She needed a plan. Could she take him back now? Of course she could, and she would (*Stupid bitch*, Lia's voice cried), but what if ... what if ... what if he wasn't there to ask to come back? What if he was going to steal even this from her?

She would have to play it cool and confident. She would tell him that she had put the house on the market (lie), and her lawyer had told her that he had no more rights to any of their stuff (lie). She would tell him that a warrant was out for him (lie) and that he shouldn't be here; she had called security (lie). She would send him away with a warning, and then she would go back to sleepwalking through her days and fitfully pacing through her nights.

Even as she told herself the fiction of being a strong, capable woman, she felt something inside drawing back. It was far more likely that he would be the one cold and confident, and she would find herself apologizing.

He was going to hit her again. She knew it—just like she knew that if she turned the handle, the water would stop coming out of the faucet. He was going to hit her, and she was going to let him.

She shivered and squeezed her eyes closed. No, she didn't have to be the quiet June; she didn't have to let him. She summoned up a mental image of Lia, her onetime role model and confidant, for inspiration. She pictured Lia's red hair aflame in the bright sunlight, her eyes flashing as she spoiled for a fight, her fists pumping, and her voice raised to an unbelievable pitch, demanding and threatening. She could be like Lia, strong and powerful.

She stood up quickly and shut off the water. In the sudden silence, her vision blurred, and she gazed blankly at the empty mirror. The reflected Pepto-Bismol-pink walls behind her rippled drunkenly, and the stall doors appeared to swing in and out as if attempting to grab her. She closed her eyes and concentrated on her breathing. One breath in, one out, another in … stupid thing, standing up so fast … and especially after another day of having nothing to eat but coffee and the obligatory staff room doughnut. She moved toward the bathroom door and pushed it open, glad to escape to the more muted colors of the hallway.

Once again in front of the elevator, she waited. The dizziness had not let up, and she felt the vague sense of impending nausea. *No,* she told herself sternly, trying to recapture the spirit if not the sound of Lia's voice. *You will not get sick. You will not let him have that effect on you.* She glared defiantly forward at the smooth metal sheen of the elevator doors as they hissed open. *You can be strong.*

And, yet, another hesitation. She glanced at her watch. It had been almost forty minutes since the phone call. Would he even still be there? Of course he would be there. This whole thing was his idea, his fault. He was the one who had finally broken the silence and sought her out. There was no way he would leave without talking to her. In fact …

Somewhere behind her a phone rang. She jumped slightly and took a half step back toward her office. Of course, she had waited so long, he was probably calling her to tell her to move her ass. But what if it was Margie, what if it was building security, what if it was a wrong number.… Ignoring Lia's whispered accusations that she was stalling, she turned away as the empty elevator doors slid shut and hurried back down the hall.

Hands shaking, she mistyped the security code and cursed softly when the door beeped at her. A small breath and she tried again, this time getting the door open and rushing toward her desk. It was still ringing ... how many rings was that now? She was almost at it when her hip connected solidly with the corner of the conference table and she pitched forward into the darkness, hitting her head on something sharp, knocking the phone onto the floor with a clatter.

Sprawled on the carpet and fighting against visions of swirling colors, she managed to bring the receiver up to her ear.

"Hello? Hello?"

Nothing but the dial tone.

Dismayed, she almost dropped the phone but managed at last to hang it up. Then, leaving the whole thing on the floor, she pulled herself to a sitting position and shook her head, blinking slowly to bring the room into focus. The office was dark, terrifyingly dark. The furniture that was normally so mundane and forgettable in the harsh florescent lights now loomed over her as questionable masses to be feared. The door had slammed shut behind her, and from her vantage point on the floor half hidden behind her desk, she could just barely make out the vague shape of Margie's large rubber plant leaning against the window.

The thought of standing made her feel ill, so she crawled over to the plant, compelled by some unknown reason to touch it, to reassure herself that even in the darkness, it had a mirror self, a bright and green and alive self that could be hers if she had the energy to turn on the light. She wanted to feel the stiff plastic leaves, to rub them against her damp palms.

At the base of the plant, she paused, distracted by the window with its cheap corporate blinds moving faintly from the air conditioning. She had an idea. On her knees, she pushed two of the slats open and peered down, down, down into the parking lot where he waited.

There he was, parked arrogantly in the handicapped spot right in front of the main doors. In the yellow parking lights he looked small and washed out. The cigarette that dangled from his fingers was nothing more than a tiny dot. From six floors up she couldn't make out much, but the nervous way he was jiggling his foot and shifting his weight back and forth told her how upset he was getting at being forced to wait.

"I can't do it," she heard herself murmur, a whispered confession.

"Yes, you can. You have to." The voice, now gentle and wise, was in her ear.

"No," she shivered, "I can't."

Suddenly, he straightened up, dropping his cigarette and, with a move so achingly familiar, stamped it out against the asphalt. He raised his hand in greeting and moved forward a few steps.

"Who's he talking to?" Lia's voice or her own, it didn't matter, the answer came anyway. "Probably nobody."

But it was a woman who had emerged from the building and now stood a few feet away from him down there in half shadow. June felt her breath catch in her throat. Whoever she was, this woman would do well to just ignore him and keep walking. *Keep walking,* she thought at the woman who was now shifting back and forth, hands pushed into heavy coat pockets.

June strained her eyes and then clamored to her feet. Who was that down there?

"Who is that?" she asked, but the voice was silent.

The woman was short, about June's height. Her hair color was hard to place in the amber light, and her body was hidden by a large black coat with a red plaid belt.

June pressed her face against the window hard, sure that she was seeing things. The woman turned toward the direction of the freeway, and for a split second, June saw her face.

"No!" She reeled back, and the blinds fell shut, plunging her back into the darkness. Backpedaling, she sat down hard on her desk and clicked on her small reading lamp. For a moment she let herself sit there, perfectly still, hearing only the breath in her chest, feeling only the pounding of her heart.

How normal her desk looked. All her papers neat and tidy, her pencils lined up, her paper clips carefully strung together. How homey she had made her desk area—photos of the cat, outdated photos of her brother's children; this was her space. If there was any doubt, there was her jacket sitting right where she had left it on the back of her chair. She had bought it on sale last December. She loved that jacket; she liked how warm and secure it made her feel. She loved the whimsy of the red plaid belt.

She closed her eyes and told herself to snap out of it. She was tired; it had been a long week; she hadn't been sleeping. There was no logical way for her to have seen what she thought she had just seen. A moment longer, and then she stood on trembling legs and walked with purpose back to the window. Before she could give herself a chance to change her mind, she pulled the blinds all the way up with a rough jerk of her wrist and looked down.

She was still there. Leaning against the car the two of them were deep in conversation. He was leaning over her, but not overly so. She was fiddling with the handle of her purse and looking up at him.

"That's me," she said dully and wasn't surprised when the answer came. "Maybe."

June started to shiver. Whole-body chills raced up and down her back. Her hands clenched in fists.

Openmouthed in shock, she watched as he leaned in and enfolded her in a hug.

"Stop!" She cried and slapped the window hard, making her arm ache. "Stop!"

He pulled back and smiled down at her, and she couldn't resist the half smile on her face as she looked back up at him.

"Stop, stop, stop," both hands now, pounding on the window. "Don't let him … he's going to … Stop!"

He stepped away from her and opened the car door.

"Don't!" Panicked, she closed her hands into fists and screamed "*Don't go with him!*"

Was that a moment of hesitation? The pressure in her head was almost blinding, and her body was taut as if all her muscles were being pulled in opposite directions. She backed away from the window and cast around for something to use.

He was smiling, all teeth, and she was hesitating in the open car door.

June lifted her desk chair and swung it at the window. She took a step back from the car, shaking her head and looking down. The legs banged against the glass and then ricocheted, hitting her hard in the mouth.

He slapped her; the smile was gone. She tasted blood. The window held.

Weeping with frustration, she leaned against it and watched. He had a hold of her arm now, his fingers tight, pulling her back.

Nothing else, she thought, *there is nothing else.* She waited, hardly hoping for Lia's voice, Lia's anger, Lia's bravado, but there was nothing but herself, her own ragged breathing, the blurred reflection of the office in the window and outside …

She wasn't struggling. The obedient victim, she was being put into the car, and he was getting ready to slam the door.

She felt a moment of calm, where everything fell into place. She took a step back and then another and another, remembering to step carefully out of her heels and over the tangled phone cords. Her breathing was calm, her eyes fixed and steady, her body coiled and ready for action, vibrating with energy. In front of her, across the expanse of corporate carpet, the window was a dark and waiting eye. She faced it.

A gentle pressure of one foot and then the other, and she was moving, moving with a grace that she had never known before, with a purpose that no amount of safety glass could contain. Head down and body tight, she did not miss.

There was a moment of shock, the glass on her skin, the cold air on her face, and then she was free.

She did not blink.

The Season

The cold wind sweeps up loose papers from an overflowing garbage can and carries them in a queer little dance down Thirty-second Street. Somewhere above, the sun prepares to go to bed, but heavy clouds have plunged the city into an early darkness, and the streets are mostly empty. Dirty snow is piled up in odd shapes, masking newspaper boxes and benches, making the landscape both terrifying and artificial. In the shelter of a bus stop, a young girl crouches. She is dirty, her hair greasy and her face smeared with snot and dried toothpaste. A large, almost faded bruise marks her left check—a reminder to behave. As the icy wind blows again, she shivers and then pats her little pocket to reassure herself that the money is still there. Mamma would be angry if it got lost. Mamma had said she may go but only if she hurried. Otherwise, Mamma would be very angry. The thought of Mamma being angry makes her shiver again, and she pulls her coat closer around her slight frame.

With a forlorn sigh she stands and plunges back onto the street. Her boots are too big, and her socks are worn through in spots, making her journey through the snow even more treacherous. Slipping and stumbling, she scurries down the street, darting from one pool of weak street light to another in sporadic bursts. It is dark and scary, and despite the thrill of responsibility, now she wants nothing more than to finish her errand and get home again.

Finally, she reaches her destination. It takes nearly all of her strength to pull open the heavy bell-laden door. Instantly, the smell of hot cinnamon, apples, and sweaty people hits her in the face like a physical blow. Staggering inside, she lets the door slam shut behind her. The heat in the small store is almost overpowering, and she feels her face flush as her vision blurs. At the register stands, a crowded line swells and moves like some gigantic creature in the throes of passion. From broken speakers, fiercely happy holiday music crackles in a futile attempt to drown out voices raised in exasperation and the shrill cries of dozens of children.

Shop girls dressed in saggy red coveralls carry boxes as they push their way through the crowds. They watch with barely hidden contempt as the last-minute shoppers rummage hungrily through bins of dented and half-off toys. In a back corner, two men stand talking in low, scratchy voices. A fight breaks out near the wooden toy department, and they watch with no expression as a woman savagely slaps her crying son and pulls a train with bright red wheels from his grubby fingers.

The little girl carefully begins to make her way through the mass of people. Her large brown eyes gaze at the toys mounted on the walls, hanging from the ceiling, and pouring from barrels that tower over her. She stops, transfixed beside a wooden carousel that nearly comes up to her knees. Riding it are little painted horses and even a double seat just like the carousel in the pictures of the summertime fair. Every year when the posters went up on the walls near the post office and the fruit stand, she would dream of going. It wasn't the Ferris wheel or the carnival games but the carousel that had caught her eye and captured her heart. She had always wanted to go to the fair, but Mamma had always said no.

She bends down until she is eye level with it and nudges an intricately carved red and black horse with a nervous but determined finger. At once, the carousel begins to spin. Her eyes light up in wonder, and she bends closer. Barely audible above the racket, she can hear the song that pours forth in tiny chiming bells. She had never heard the song before, but it seems to be just what a real carousel would play. She closes her eyes to hear it better.

Around her, the sounds of the store carry on. She bites her lip, spins the carousel again, and concentrates. She can hear the beeping of the cash register. Near her left ear a baby is crying into its mother's shoulder. A man's voice can be heard saying, "I think this is the one." The sweet bell music is playing and ...

Boom!

She tips forward and to the right and lands with a moan on the hard floor. The mother, still cooing to her baby, looks down nastily at the girl sprawled on the floor.

"Stupid girl! Don't you know better than to sit where people are walking?"

Her voice is sharp, and it makes the little girl tremble.

"Yes, ma'am," she mumbles, climbing awkwardly to her feet.

The woman glares at her a second longer as the baby unleashes a new volley of outraged screams, and then she turns on her heel and stomps away. The little girl sighs in gratitude that she had been so easily dealt with and turns back to the carousel. Instead she sees a man staring down at her with wicked amusement. He bends down and takes her roughly by the shoulders. He smells of sour milk, and it is all she can do to not wrinkle up her nose and strain to pull away.

"What's your name, little girl?" he sneers at her in a voice ruined by alcohol and age.

"P-P-Pattie," she stutters, her voice showing her fear and confusion.

"Well, Pattie, my name's Vic, and this here's Lou." Pattie pulls her eyes from his dark ones and looks at his partner. Her lip begins to tremble.

"Hi, Pattie." Lou's voice is just as scratchy as Vic's. Pattie looks back at Vic.

"Your mamma sent us to come get you, Pattie. It's getting late, and it's time for you to come home."

Mamma? Was it that late already? Was Mamma angry with her? Is that why she had sent these two men to get her? Pattie's eyes fill with tears.

"Now don't you cry. Just come along with us and be a good girl."

In a daze of fear and perplexity, she allows herself to be led from the store and back into the blistering cold.

The only person who noticed the odd confrontation was the mother whose baby had mercifully decided to sleep. She wondered briefly what those men were doing to that girl, but she still had shopping to do and young ones at home. Besides, what was the worst that could happen?

Surface Dweller

We went back to her place because it was closer and because I was legitimately interested in seeing her art. Sleeping with her, sure, but art was what had brought me out to the gallery opening on such a rainy night in the first place, and art had been the focus of our conversation for at least an hour before it dawned on me that she might be interested in more than just my ranting about the importance of oil paints as an aesthetic choice. Her overzealous and almost painful exuberance in the cab ride had not only embarrassed the driver but had also made her intentions obvious.

We had met by the Caspian piece, hung in its typical style in the back corner. I have always admired his work, and his insistence on his paintings being hung too high for close inspection has always filled me with a sort of sardonic glee. This painting—big, horrible sunflowers— was no exception. It hung almost too close to the lights, inviting the uninformed to crane their necks. Those of us in the know stood across the room. She was in the know. We had shared a glance and brief nod of recognition as she took her place beside me, glass of white wine held loosely in her hand.

We stood in silence for several moments, and then she gasped.

"Are you okay?" I moved a step closer, an unconscious response that brought me near enough to smell her perfume—pleasant, but nothing special.

"Oh, yes," she laughed, a faint blush moving up her face. "I just finally saw it, you know, what's really there. It always takes me a few minutes, and then sometimes it's a surprise."

I smiled to show I understood and turned back to the flowers that were joyfully strangling each other in an orgy of violence, petals falling, stems pulled taut, small beads of dew (perspiration?) flying through the air.

"I sometimes wonder if someday he'll paint something that's just what it is. Just the surface, you know?" She continued talking, and, surprised, I turned back to her, "… and if people will stand around and look and look and maybe even make things up or try really hard to find the darker meaning when there isn't one."

Her cheeks were flushed, and she waved her hands around to emphasize her point. Thankfully, her wine glass was empty.

I took the final sip from my own glass (a heavy dark cab) and a closer look at her. At first glance, she looked like half the women there; navy skirt, white blouse over something dark and lacey, high, insensible heels, and a series of silver bracelets. Her face was open and inviting; her figure was pleasant but nothing special. I was ready to walk away, go back to the bar, maybe even leave, but her next statement changed all that.

"I'm the third from the left, you know."

"Pardon?"

"In the painting," she clarified as she raised her empty glass to her lips, realized it was empty, and lowered her arm with well-practiced nonchalance.

I looked back at the flowers, the faceless, glistening flowers, then at her questioningly.

"Well," she laughed, a full-bodied laugh that was bawdy and innocent all at once, "At least that's what he told me. I think he must tell that to all his students."

"You're a Caspian student?" I tried to keep the shock out of my voice. I had always pictured his students as older, as very sophisticated, as … male.

"Yeah," she shrugged, "but I'm not sure for how long. He's so temperamental, and my stuff isn't deep enough for him. All I see is the surface." She looked down at her glass again as if to reassure herself that it was empty and then smiled up at me.

"Carrie, my name," she extended her hand.

I shook it, feeling the calluses of a serious artist and smiled back. "I'm Beth."

She lived in a tiny series of rooms on the fourth floor in a typical New York walk-up, meaning that we walked up four flights of stairs. She led the way, rear end swinging and heels clacking loud enough to wake the dead, or at least half her neighbors. Inside, she locked the door behind us, sliding the bolt in place with a flick of her wrist. Apparently, I would be spending the night.

By the light from the street below and the wrought-iron lamp on the coffee table, she showed me her pieces. She dealt mainly in vague shapes and colors, and her work was indeed all surface, cliché moments of tragedy. I counted five "death scenes" and seven "violence against young girl" pieces. There was one graveyard scene that was slightly more interesting, but even it had the aged look of something copied from something else. She remained silent during my inspection, but knowing my role, I made the appropriate sounds of interest.

"Well," she waved dismissively when I had finished and leaned them back up against the coffee table, "what you really want to see is in the bedroom."

"I don't know," I said, looking down at her sprawled out on the floor, propped up on one elbow with the lamplight casting shadows on her neck. The hem of her skirt had ridden up, exposing the top tips of lacy stockings. "I rather like what I can see in here."

She laughed and trailed her fingers across her knee. "Right, sure, but really, you ought to go have a look. I'll get some wine."

In one graceful motion, she stood and moved toward the kitchen, her feet a whisper on the carpet (the heels having been removed in haste before even her coat half an hour before). I followed and caught her around the waist, kissing the back of her neck, "Forget the wine."

"Are you sure? You might wish you had some before we go back there." She ran her nails over my arm. Pleasant, but … I caught her hands in mine and turned her around to face me. "Nope, I'm good."

She blinked up at me slowly, and for a minute I thought she had changed her mind about everything, but then she gently grasped my wrists and, walking backward, led me down the dark hallway.

Her bedroom was small, the furniture crowded up against itself to create that wholesome claustrophobic feeling only found in small apartments. An entire wall was taken up with a canvas that had been covered by a stained drop cloth. As she lit candles and a joint, I glanced through her window at the brick-wall view.

"Are you ready?" Her voice was a bit tenser than before, and when I turned around, she was standing in front of the wall piece staring at me with an intensity that was beyond brazen. The combination of incense and weed had already begun to fill the room, the scent heavy and cloying. Before I could respond, she turned and pulled the cloth off, revealing what had been hidden.

I gasped and stumbled back, hitting my hip on her dresser. The images (faces, screaming faces) swam before my eyes, moving and dancing in the flickering candlelight. I blinked long and hard, sure I had been mistaken and then looked again. It wasn't any better. The disjointed feeling of extreme dizziness descended. I shut my eyes and turned away, my hands groping for the window. Fresh air. I needed fresh air.

"You don't like it?" Her voice was deep and monotone.

"It's ... it's ... very powerful stuff ..." With my eyes still closed, I fumbled with the window, desperate for the latch. I could feel the painting behind me, an almost palpable presence in this tiny room that was full of smoke.

"You hardly looked at it." There was an edge in her voice now, and I felt her eyes in the small of my back pushing into me.

"No? Oh, I'll look again," I risked opening my eyes and was instantly nauseous. Squinting, I could see the lock on the window. Painted shut.

I leaned my head against the glass, trying to trick myself into believing that it was cool, and took a gasping breath, almost gagging on the fumes. Bracing myself and looking everywhere except at the painting, I turned around to face her.

She was standing in front of it (them), the candlelight casting furious shadows over her face. For a moment she was the painting, and it was her—all big, dark eyes and savage mouth. I groaned and closed my eyes again.

"Look at it! Look at me!"

Where was the door? The smoke was strangling me, and I could feel my sweat in thick, slick trails down my back. I took a hesitant step forward, hands outstretched, eyes squeezed tight. In front of me, she, it, they loomed.

Suddenly, her hands were on my face. Her touch burnt, and I whimpered and tried to pull away, but she held on and pushed me down until I was kneeling, knees on the carpet, my own hands on her wrists, trying to pull away, failing. Her thumbs dug into my cheeks, nails breaking the skin, and her breath molten in my face.

"Look, damn you. *Look!*"

"Please, oh god, please let me …"

More pressure from her nails, then blood joined the sweat on my face. Her lips against mine, wet with spittle, now a whisper that seemed to echo. "Open your eyes, or I'll carve them out of your head."

I obeyed, a sob catching in my throat. Her eyes were from mine, wide and dilated. Behind her the painting hovered like a sick dream, drowning out everything else, mocking from the shadows.

"Do you see? Do you see what I am? What I can do?" Her voice was manic, and despite the crushing heat, I was suddenly cold.

"Yes, I see. I see. Carrie, you're hurting me …"

Her hands loosened. She let go suddenly and took a step back. I fell forward and instinctively reached for my face, feeling the small crescent-shaped cuts. Weak and sick, I huddled in a heap. The only sound in the room was my hoarse sobbing.

When nothing happened, I forced myself to look up at her, at them, and felt my blood freeze in my veins. She stood, her back to me, facing it, and it … it shimmered and swayed above her. Floating in front of her, the painted eyes and lips opening and closing. It was her face, again and again, twisted and angry; it was my face, marked and terrified. It was faces of strangers, of lovers, faces of pain, bleeding on each other and laughing. There was a rush of blood in my head, and for a moment I thought I could hear them—hear them laughing, screaming, crying, pleading. Then I realized it was my own voice—it was me; I was weeping, begging her to make them stop even while I screamed at myself to look away but couldn't. My voice, mangled and weak, joining with the crescendo of wailing and the moving, blinking lids and drooling, slack-jawed mouths, my own nails digging into my cheeks, trying to find a way to stop looking … to stop seeing …

She darted forward, pulled up the drop cloth, and it was gone. I blinked at the stained cloth, knowing what lay behind it, and felt my heart beating wildly in my neck. In the sudden silence I could hear myself breathing, and I realized I could breathe easily again. The incense must have burnt out, and the smell of her joint was gone as well. She stood by her vanity, her reflection gazing quietly at me through the mirror, her hair moving softy in the breeze from the open window.

I pivoted and crawled on trembling limbs for the door. In the hallway I scrambled to my feet, ignoring the loss of a shoe, and scurried toward the living room. It was dark, and I tripped over the coffee table, hitting my head on some dark piece of furniture and sprawling on the floor. Panting and dizzy with fright, I tried to get up, but my legs were too weak and tangled together. Sobbing, I collapsed again.

"Here, let me help you." She was beside me, her hands cool and soft, her voice the sweet, rich sound I had heard at the gallery. I stifled a scream and pulled away, "No! Don't touch me! Get away!"

She recoiled as if slapped but then recovered and came at me again. I made several futile attempts to slap her hands away. She half carried, half dragged me to the couch and leaned me up against it. Leaving me there, she went into the kitchen and soon came the unmistakable sounds of her putting the kettle on and opening and closing cupboard doors.

I looked forlornly across the room at the front door, still bolted, and tried to muster up the strength to crawl or drag myself toward it. It seemed to retreat from my gaze, the distance across the floor growing longer every second. I shut my eyes and felt the weight of exhaustion pulling at me. I concentrated on my breathing—in … out … in … out—and realized from a long, long way away that I was too tired to move.

Something cold and wet was on my forehead, and I forced my eyes to open. She knelt beside me, washcloth in hand. Her eyes devoid of expression, she washed my face and then lifted a coffee mug of some steaming liquid to my lips. I tried to turn my head away, but it, like the rest of me, was terribly heavy and unresponsive. She tipped my head back and poured a few swallows of the Earl Grey tea down my throat. I felt its warmth all the way down, and I shivered.

She perched a few feet away from me and drank her own tea. I watched her expectantly through half-closed lids.

"You'll be okay, you know." Her voice was soft, apologetic, but her body was still wooden, tense. "Tomorrow you'll wake up, and you might not even remember what you saw."

My eyes were trying to close again. I fought against the dark, silent pull of sleep.

She continued, looking at me but not really seeing me at all. "You'll remember exactly what you want, a reality based on what you thought you would see and feel. A casual one-night stand with some random art student … pleasant but nothing special …"

"What … what did you do to me??" It was a whisper, but I knew she heard me.

"Me? Nothing. I just showed you what was under the surface. The stuff you don't see at first, not until you look closer. The things only you can see."

She moved closer, wrapping her arm around my shoulder and cradling me against her chest. Her fingers in my hair, her voice soft, "Sometimes, it takes a while, but not you. You saw it right away."

The desire to relax, to sleep here with her, was overwhelming, but inwardly I struggled against it. She leaned down and kissed my cheek like a mother, like an angel. Her lips rested against my skin, and her voice was faint, a gentle singsong:

"What did you see, Angel Beth? When you looked under the surface, beyond where the flowers can grow, what did you see?"

My lips against her breast, eyelashes against her skin, the steady beat of her heart in my ear, I couldn't help but whisper back, the word pulled from me by invisible nylon ropes.

"… myself."

She leaned back, satisfied, still holding me lovingly, her hands gentle and soothing. Outside, a truck passed by, its heavy, thudding tires rumbling at us through the windows. Inside somewhere a clock ticked, and I listened to her breathe, knowing that I would be asleep at any moment, powerless to fight it anymore and almost relieved to be able to escape. I let myself sink into her, felt the tension leave my body as I surrendered.

"Sometimes, it's a surprise."

Goals

There has to be a goal. That's what life is after all, a series of goals that we meet or we don't. One could judge a life of success versus failure all on which goals were met and which were not.

That summer the air was always warm, and the pavement was always hot under our feet. We were twenty-two, and we felt like the world wasn't just our oyster but our motherfucking *oyster bar,* man. It seemed okay to break down all of existence into good and bad, big and little, goal met or goal denied.

Brett and I were two such guys—well, he would have called us "blokes" because earlier that summer he had adopted an annoying British persona. He swore it helped him pick up chicks. All I could see it did was make waitresses laugh at us and bartenders roll their eyes. It also made it almost impossible to understand him once he got drunk, and he got drunk every night. So did I. This was our time, our shining moment. Brett said to waste it would be not only a crime against our inner children but against all of nature itself.

This was our last free summer, and we intended to maximize our experience. When we talked about it in May, about all the fine girls we would bang and the great booze we would drink, it had seemed like the perfect plan. But by the end of June, I was having second thoughts. We had drunk a lot of booze, but I wasn't sure how good most of it had been. Brett was the only one getting laid, and the girls weren't really all that fine.

"Danny, old chap, you have to relax. You're always too uptight; the ladies don't like that." These were Brett's sage words of wisdom to me, which he would deliver five or six times throughout the night as we sat at the bar in the Mix or walked to the Puddle or hovered around the outskirts of the frantic dancers at the Café. I didn't like that he called me Danny—my name is Daniel—or that he added in that "old chap" bit. I was actually only about four hours older than him. This fact had been discovered during our first semester at State and had created the type of bond that was destined to last all four years of college. As for me being uptight, I didn't agree with that at all. I just tend to be more on the outside of things. Brett always wants to—no, needs to—be in the very center. He's the type who likes to talk too loud because it is his belief that his personal conversation is massively more important and interesting than whatever anyone else could possibly be talking about at the time.

He also tends to invite random people into whatever conversation he is having.

"Wouldn't you agree, luv?" he asks the waitress who has just delivered us plates of eggs, bacon, and pancakes punctuated with tiny, perfectly shaped mounds of butter. The drinking part of the night is over for the evening. Because neither one of us got laid tonight, we are here at this Denny's trying to sober up enough to drive back to the suburbs. The waitress doesn't agree or disagree; she probably can't tell which one of us will be paying and doesn't want to screw herself out of a nice tip. She just smiles.

She has a nice smile, and her breasts under her uniform blouse suddenly remind me of the little mounds of butter on my pancakes. I blush, sure that she can read my mind, and fumble for the Tabasco sauce. Brett, who is always bitter when he doesn't even get a girl's number for the night, has apparently decided to make our waitress the object of his stunted lust. He isn't going to let her get away without picking sides in our imagined argument. Before she had come over to our table, we had been halfheartedly talking about the lack of good music at the clubs. This was an old conversation and one in which we pretty much agreed that whatever "house" techno was, it sucked the big one. Not really a philosophical discussion for the record books and certainly not something I wanted to bring her into.

"No, really, luv." He reaches out and takes her hand. Only Brett could grab an unknown waitress' hand and make it look suave and romantic instead of creepy and chauvinistic. "Wouldn't you agree?"

It is her turn to blush, and when she does, she also looks down and slightly to the side. She has a mole on her neck, a little bit of darkness on her skin. I find myself wondering what her other bits of darkness look like. Brett is gently running his fingers over the top of her hand, waiting for a response. She shrugs and pulls her hand away. A moment later, she, her mole, and her butter-mound breasts are gone, and it is just us with the soggy pancakes.

Brett watches the swinging kitchen door she had escaped into for a moment, a concentrated look of disappointment on his face just in case she had glanced behind her or is even now peeking out at our table. Then, satisfied that he has laid down the foundation for an eventual seduction, he turns to his breakfast and starts to shovel scrambled eggs into his mouth.

Any of the girls that Brett lays this summer would be disgusted to see him eat. He attacks his food with a gusto normally reserved for those starving third-world country children or middle-aged women cheating on some horrible diet. Brett eats as if he has never had the chance to finish a meal before, as if at any moment his food might be taken away from him. I asked him once if he had a whole slew of siblings, attributing his eating habits to a long-suffering risk of not getting enough. I was pretty confident in my explanation of Brett's eating habits; I felt it not only explained his attitude toward his food but also why no one had ever coached him on proper table etiquette. His mother probably hadn't had the time with so many children.

When I had asked Brett about his plethora of siblings, I had been intending to inwardly congratulate myself on my keen psychological analysis. Brett, though, had been confused by my question, our friendship never before delving into such an intimate subject before, and had told me that he was an only child. Crushed, I gave up trying to figure out a logical reason for anything Brett did and instead simply allowed myself to be entertained by his antics.

Regardless of why he ate in the disgusting way he did, with specks of food flying out of his open mouth and the occasional bite being moved from plate to mouth with his hands as if he had forgotten that he knew how to use a fork or a spoon, his obvious enjoyment of the process made it hard for me to condemn him as a slob. When we were newly friends, I had watched him eat with a mixture of awe and revulsion. He never noticed, so intent was he on his food. Eventually, though, I had to stop watching, or I would lose my own appetite. Hearing him eat was bad enough.

Brett was the type of guy who constantly mumbled (or downright talked) to himself. It was always with such vivid intensity that one was loath to interrupt. Eating was no exception. He talked as he ate and grunted at his food. I imagine that he mumbled his way through sex as well and always felt a bit bad for the girls he took home. What did they make of his constant jabbering? Although, considering that he talked so much and still managed to get girls to go home with him and I hardly ever talked and hardly ever got girls to come home with me, maybe girls like being mumbled at.

I eat my pancakes without butter. I move the little blobs off to the side where I can watch them slowly melt while I pretend to not care that our waitress has emerged from the kitchen and is taking orders from a very loud table in the back of the room. That table, full of giggly girls with high-pitched laughs, seems to be ordering an awful lot of food. Our waitress (yes, she is ours, at least as long as we are here, and I do indeed feel a bit possessive toward her) writes quickly as the girls throw out food requests like "no avocados" and "ranch on the side." They aren't even ordering their food in order, just peppering our waitress with names of entrées and desserts, and she is hunched over her waitress pad, scribbling. Part of her ponytail has slipped out, and she brushes a bit of hair out of her face.

"So, mate, gonna try to meet that goal after all?" Brett has finished his food and has noticed me noticing our waitress. This is his thing right now, this goal thing. Every night as we set off he makes goals—goals for him and goals for me. *One shouldn't go out, one shouldn't drink, and one should most definitely not have sex without a goal in mind*, he lectures me as some random bartender brings us our first drink of the night. We usually start off with mixed cocktails because it makes us feel adult to order things like White Russians and vodka gimlets. By the end of the night, we transition back to the comfort of cheap beer. Our conversation ebbs and flows, but it always gets back to the goals.

Brett's goals are always the same: Go out to get drunk. Get drunk enough to have a good time and forget that September is only a couple of months away. Get laid. My goals are usually recycled as well: Go out to have a good time. Drink. Drink until I won't mind not getting laid. Get laid? Well, that would be great, but I know better than to make that an actual goal. I say this to him almost every night, but he knows that getting laid is one of my goals. It is my unspoken goal. So far this summer I haven't even gotten close.

Brett is watching our waitress now, his eyes alert and bright. The booze seems to have worn off completely. I hate his ability to sober up so fast. It has been forty-five minutes since we stumbled out of whatever club we had been at when the first cries of "last call" had started, but I still feel swollen, and my tongue is slightly too big for my mouth. "She's pretty posh there, mate. Might be worth a spin or two." He seems to have forgotten that he wanted her a moment ago, and when he turns back to me, he is leering. I politely tell him to fuck off. He feigns deep hurt and then throws his napkin (still clean) on the table and gets up. "Off to the loo; need to have a bit o' a piss."

Alone, I survey the dirty plates. In my still slightly drunken state, I am sure there are cryptic meanings in the syrup patterns. The butter blobs have become a buttery goo that is undistinguishable from any of the other puddles of sticky residue. I stare down at the leftovers of our 3:00 AM breakfast and wish there was meaning in it. All it is, I tell myself morosely, is the leavings of two idiots who are trying to drink away their fear of the real world. The mess on the table is the evidence of our whole pathetic existence: just another night, just like last night and tomorrow night, full of bars and beers and then eating breakfast at some all-night diner before going home and passing out. There is a shadow over the half-eaten eggs (I can never finish my eggs), and it takes me a moment to realize it isn't a metaphor. I look up; my waitress has brought us the check.

Is that pity in her eyes (hazel, by the way), or is she just tired of stupid half-drunken "blokes" who come in here to wrap up their nights? I would hate her job. I want to tell her that I appreciate her and the hundreds of other waitresses who bookend these blurry adventures for us. After the garishly done-up girls at the clubs—the ones with the short skirts, way too much makeup, the tight blouses with hard, pointy nipples—I like to see a pretty waitress in tennis shoes with her hair sort of messy and her eyes tired and kind.

She is standing here, sort of half looking at me and half looking at the table. I feel embarrassed for the mess we have left on our plates, as if we should have eaten everything so there would be less for her to have to carry back to the kitchen, less of a mess for her to have to deal with. She fumbles in her apron pocket for our bill, reads it over quickly, and then puts it down close to the edge but equal distance from me and Brett's empty chair. She isn't presuming to know which one of us will pay. I like her even more for this careful consideration. It is horrible to be handed the check and then have to pass it over to someone else; I always feel like a cheap schmuck. She will leave now, I realize; her tenure as my waitress is almost complete. We will take the check to the cashier, a dour-looking woman who glared at us when we came in, and then we will leave, and I won't ever see her again. I desperately try to think of something to say, something to keep her here for another minute or two.

"Sorry about my friend." My voice is loud, too loud, and it makes her jump a little. She recovers quickly, though, and smiles at me again. "I mean," I go on, full of drunken babble and wishing very much that I could stop myself, "He didn't mean to grab you or anything. He's kinda a schmuck, but harmless. Not like me." What the hell did that mean? What did I just say? "I mean, not the being harmless thing; I'm harmless too. I meant the schmuck thing." Her smile gets bigger and she nods, but I am worried she still might not get what I'm trying to say. "I'm not a schmuck." Then, because I actually kind of feel like one right now, "Well, not usually anyway." I turn my face to the wall and wait for the earth to open up and swallow me whole.

The wall is boring, no clever wallpaper or interesting pattern in the paint or anything, and I know I won't be able to keep looking at it for very long. There is a slight pressure on my arm, and I turn back. Her hand is on my elbow. She isn't looking at me, just kind of off into the distance.

"I get off at five o'clock." Then she moves away quickly as if embarrassed and disappears again through the kitchen door.

* * *

At 5:13, I am back. I know that I'm late; it took longer than it should have to get Brett off to bed. After Denny's, he had been in an annoyingly chatty mood. Eventually, he talked himself to sleep, and I had thrown my clothes back on and drove like a madman to the restaurant, praying that she would still be there.

She is sitting on one of the little benches they put out in front of the doors next to the newspaper machines and the overflowing ashtray. Wearing a jean jacket over her uniform, she stops swinging her feet when the headlights hit her. Her ponytail is slung forward around her neck, hiding her mole. When I walk up, she smiles at me. It's a shy smile, and I know I am grinning back like an idiot.

We go to her place; it's only a few blocks away. "Walking distance," she says, but I insist on driving. It makes me feel chivalrous to open her door, and for a moment I am proud of my car (bought my junior year of high school with money from my first job) until I remember that I drive Brett around. I apologize over and over again for the mess and am glad that the darkness makes it hard to see the backseat, where Brett has a habit of throwing anything and everything. There are magazines, empty brown paper bags, discarded soda bottles, a few dog-eared maps, and an assortment of pens and notebooks on the seats. I don't even want to hazard a guess to what's on the floor back there. She assures me that she doesn't mind and directs me to her apartment building.

It is a studio, with her bed pushed into a corner like an afterthought. The windows had been left open. The air is cool and smells like trees. She makes herself a pot of tea and butters toast while I survey the books on her shelves and try not to stare at her. She sits on the floor with her bread and eats in quick birdlike bites. I enjoy the carefulness with which she holds each piece, the delicate movement of her throat as she swallows. We make small talk without looking at each other, but I can sense her nervousness. Her cheeks are faintly red.

When she is done eating, she washes her hands and lights the tall, red candle that sits precariously on her dresser. In the semidark we undress, stealing glances at each other. We lie down together on her tiny bed, and suddenly the timidness is gone. She kisses me like she is starving, and I run my hands over her skin, exploring every inch. I was right; her breasts are small, round mounds, sweet and soft. Her hair, when it is down, is long, and in the candlelight, her eyes are deep.

When we are done, I lie perfectly still, listening to her breathe through her nose. The candle has gone out, and the sun is up, shining through the open windows and flooding the room with bright white light. I move to get up, but she wraps her arms around me and pulls me back down. I let her hold me until she falls asleep, and then I get up, grab my clothes, and leave, shutting the door softly.

Outside, the city is already awake and getting hot. The Sacramento heat doesn't know enough to wait for the afternoons but will suffocate you with thick oppression even at seven o'clock in the morning. When it is this hot, this early, you just know that the late afternoon will be unbearable. I get in my car and drive home, doing my best to avoid thinking.

It only takes me twenty minutes to pack. In Crescent City it won't be as hot, and besides, my dad could probably use a hand around the store. I pin a note to Brett's chest, "Gone home, be back before school starts," then get back in the car. Headed north on the freeway, I blast Van Halen and try to stay awake.

Wife

Eventually, Jake came to see where she had gone and found her sitting silently in the spare bedroom, half hidden behind the unpacked boxes and staring blankly into the distance. From the doorway he asked her if she was okay. Leslie responded automatically and without emotion. Oblivious to the fresh tears on her cheeks, he had no reason to doubt her sincerity and left her there in the lightless room, returning to his guests.

They were, of course, his guests because this was, of course, his house. Leslie listened to them talk and laugh in the other room as the sun slowly sank behind the hills and left her isolated in the dark. Soon the dimness crept into the other rooms of the house, and she could hear the men turning on lights and shutting doors and windows against the chill of the night.

They would be hungry soon. She knew that her absence would eventually be noticed, and she would be sought out from her hiding spot in order to make and serve dinner. She had been looking forward to serving them dinner. It was one of the ways she showed that she was a good Wife, but as she sat in the dark, she couldn't make herself feel anything but hate for this man that she was supposed to love; a quick flare-up that was gone almost as quickly as it had come.

Her momentary flash of bitterness made her feel ashamed. She was lucky, and she knew it. But it wasn't like she had planned to simply be a Wife, even if it was to one of the richest men in Missouri. He was still a "man's man," all hard grime and sweat, nothing like the soft upper-class gentlemen of California. Although, she hadn't exactly planned on being a Wife to any of those men either. Back in Bakersfield, she had been rather set on becoming an attorney or a businesswoman, a Citizen once she could get the money together, someone who wore suits and nylons to work and who knew how to order wine in fancy restaurants. That was before Joel, before Cris. That was before this.

There was a slam in the kitchen, and instinctually she got up off the floor, and she quickly shoved the soft silk and what was left of the rose into a garbage bag. A quick flick of her wrists, and the bag was tied shut, ready to be thrown out later. Closing the door behind her, she stepped, blinking, into the light of the other room. She pushed thoughts of what she had found out of her mind; the men were in the kitchen doing who knows what. It might be his house, but she felt a certain amount of protectiveness for the pots and pans she had recently purchased. (All of his had been cracked and stained, and it had been easy to convince him to let her buy new things.) Her delight with the crockery was one of the ways she knew that she had settled. Like her excitement for the new scented dish soap, she felt both thrilled and secretly ashamed that this was now her life.

She found them gathered around the table. One of the Tims was stacking empty beer cans into a pyramid while Jake and the other Tim, the shorter one, were watching in anticipation. She paused in the doorway to take in the scene: cans on the table and chairs, paper plates (greasy from the pizza they had devoured for lunch) on the floor and countertops, an unnamable part of an engine resting on the stove as if it belonged there, and faint black smudges all over the hands and foreheads of the men. A quick glance told her there were black smudges on the walls and cabinet handles of her kitchen as well.

Leslie wanted to scream. To charge across the room and with one push send the beer pyramid (now almost a dozen levels high) crashing to the ground. It would be loud, it would be frightening, it would catch them off guard, and it would be fun. Instead, she pulled a rubber band from her jeans pocket and absently tied up her hair, slipping back into her almost familiar role.

"Y'all got grease over evra' thang." She moved through the room stacking plates, clucking to herself, turning on the water in the sink, delivering her lines with mock aggravation. "Now, git yer big, manly stuff outta my kitchen so I can make some dinner."

There was the expected grumbling as they filed out of the room, the short Tim casually lifting whatever it was off the stove and carrying it away with ease. The last to leave was Jake, who gave her an approving nod before the door swung shut.

Alone, she listened to them in the garage. There was the clang of the tools, the murmur of voices, the occasional vibrating whine of some piece of machinery. Man sounds. She turned her attention to cleaning the kitchen, moving through the echo of her words as she washed and wiped and put to order. This was her kitchen; she had claimed it.

She pulled chicken from the freezer and while it defrosted, gathered ingredients out of the cupboards. Sesame crackers, garlic salt, pepper; from the fridge, the butter; from the rack above the stove, the cooking oil. Her body went through the motions while her mind flew a thousand miles away to another kitchen. Well, no, she told herself; it was actually a bit more than a thousand miles. It was exactly 1,857 miles from here to her old kitchen. She knew; she had looked it up as if knowing the exact distance would make it easier to forget. But 1,857 miles wasn't enough. Being in the country instead of the city wasn't enough. She was six states away but still making the same thing for dinner. She closed her eyes tight and took a deep breath. A beat to collect herself, and then she forced her eyes to glaze over, and she returned to the task at hand.

Later, she lay under him and tried to look through the ceiling toward the stars. From the open window the moon shone through the branches of the trees, making strange patterns over the bed. In the city they had been forced to always keep the windows shut and the curtains drawn tight in order to avoid the artificial red light that bathed all the streets. There had been hardly any trees, and no one could see the stars. But Leslie always imagined them there, high above, looking down on her. In her dreams they were angels trapped high above the harsh city lights, watching everyone in silent sympathy.

She whispered his name when he came, just the way she knew he liked her to, as if she too had found release, letting her voice drawl and lift in a mockery of his accent. Like everything else that was false now, she hardly noticed. Afterward, he slept hard as he always did: head back, mouth open, body thick, heavy, and covered in a sheer layer of sweat. Tense and awake, she let her mind wander back to the rose.

She had been halfheartedly cleaning, letting the afternoon sun light the room and watching with vague interest as the dust danced across the hardwood floor. He had moved into this house five months ago, but there still was what seemed like a cardboard army of unopened boxes stacked in the empty rooms, waiting. Her things had all fit into two suitcases. When she had arrived last month, she had unpacked them frantically as if the sooner her clothes were in drawers the sooner the whole thing would be real. All she had brought with her were clothes. Per the instructions, she had left everything else in her apartment behind to gather dust or be auctioned off. She didn't really know; she didn't really care. Sometimes she thought about home, a concept she wasn't fully able to shake, that somewhere else had been a true home, a place of safety and security and hope. That place had been home, and this place was just where she was now, no matter how many new pans she bought or how much space she took up in the dresser.

She spent her days cleaning and working in the garden, an unholy plot of dry dirt and optimism in the backyard. When the monotony threatened to drive her crazy, she would unpack a box of his things, pulling items of mystery or clothing from bygone decades out into the light. Sometimes she asked him what he wanted her to do with this or that, and he would shrug as if he didn't care and go back to his work. So she arranged things, organized things, washed and ironed and hung things up. She told herself she was making this place where they were into a home.

Occasionally, but not often, he would take things down and throw them away. The painting of the sailboat she had found and hung with a sense of pride in the bathroom disappeared the next day, and she found it buried in the trash. Another day, she found a small, hand-carved wooden figurine of a little boy playing with a puppy. She had set it on the windowsill of the dining room only to find it broken and discarded a few days later. She never asked about these items; she knew her role.

Today, she had found what she hadn't realized she had been looking for in every box: some of Angie's things. She had reached lazily into a large, unlabeled white box and had pulled out a soft, silky white nightgown, the lace yellowing, the straps uneven. It was the sort of thing a grandmother would give a Bride, and for a moment she saw Angie as she must have looked wearing it and felt a stab of envy. She knew about Angie. He had never bothered to hide it from her—just like he knew about Joel and the baby and the other car and the law office and the debt. It went without saying that the past was what had brought them here. It wasn't supposed to matter anymore. And it hadn't, until today.

She lifted the negligee from the box and let it slide between her fingers taking a perverse pleasure in knowing that her hands were dirty, covered in cardboard-box grime. She pressed it against her cheek and inhaled, wanting to find a scent to go along with the faceless woman who had been Jake's Bride, but it smelled of nothing more than old paper.

She balled it up on her lap and peered anxiously into the box, her heart beating rapidly for the first time since she had arrived here. She didn't want to admit it, but she hoped she would find a forgotten photo or letter or remnant, some clue as to the woman she was supposed to replace. The box was full of documents in manila folders. Breaking the unspoken rule about personal papers, she pored over them looking for something, but they were just farming reports, legal notes about the property in Napa, long ledgerlike tallies of soil production. As she read them, each and every one, she stroked the silk on her lap, enjoying the sensation of something so soft.

There had been plenty of silk nightgowns at the Kohl's department store back in Bakersfield. When she went with the money the agency sent her to buy things for the move, she had walked past them over and over again, trying to decide. She hadn't wanted to take any of her own clothing; it seemed wrong somehow. So she had purchased new underwear, socks, jeans, shirts, one nice dress for church, a few sweaters for the chilly nights, and a small collection of toiletries. She wanted to be able to get off the plane as someone new, someone unfettered with the past. Wasn't that the whole point?

She had been fine during the shopping trip until spotting the sleepwear section of the store. The idea of what to wear to bed had brought her up short. She knew that sleeping together was part of the arrangement. She had gone through the medical examination, her cheeks on fire, answering the questions as honestly as possible. Yes, she liked regular sex. No, she didn't feel the need to experiment. Yes, she would be a willing lover to the Husband (Jake). No, she would not deviate from the regiment of birth control. Yes, she understood what was expected of her. No, she didn't have any illusions. And she had been prepared for the coupling. She had been briefed on what he liked; she knew the layout of his bedroom. They had even told her which side of the bed she would occupy.

No one had told her what she should wear.

Standing in the store, her arms full of fashionless clothes—clothes fit for staying inside, staying out of the way, keeping the house clean and the meals made—she had started to panic. It all had been so carefully arranged, so systematically organized that she had moved through the process easily, never missing a step or an appointment or a conversation. At that stage in the process, Jake called once a day at 4:00 on the dot, and she listened to him talk about the shop and the land and the house, the phone muted, her hands clenched, her mind open, trying to learn his language, his rhythm and meter of speech. She tried to memorize his accent, and after the line went dead, she would always practice it over and over again so that when she spoke at last to him at the airport it would be perfect, and he would be pleased. The thought of failing, of having him be unsatisfied and returning her was almost more than she could contemplate, so she practiced, she read all the brochures, and she told herself she would get it right. Everything was a preparation; everything was planned. And then suddenly she had been faced with a decision where she didn't have a worksheet to refer to or a glossy manual to assist her. For the first time since the process had begun, she had felt powerless.

After changing her mind and then changing it back, she had at last settled on a long cotton nightgown with spaghetti straps. It was black with tiny dark blue flowers, and the fabric was soft but not sexual. In the end it hadn't mattered. He liked to take her clothes off with the light still on (she had come to think of this as the worst part) and then hurriedly click it off and couple with her in a sort of frantic haste. When he was done, he would fall asleep with one heavy arm pinning her down, and she would lie shivering beside him. In the mornings, he would wake her with another round of coupling and seemed to be frustrated if she had covered herself in the night. Staying nude made it easier. Some mornings she tried to fool herself into thinking that she was just dreaming it, that she wasn't here at all, that the man inside her was Joel.

But it wasn't the nightgown that had made her cry. In the next box, full of more papers and meaningless reports, Leslie found a binder that held yearly accounting information for another farm in California. In the space between the rings there was a single dried red rose.

It lay in her hand, a bud about to open and frozen forever. It didn't smell like a rose; it hardly even looked like one, and the ribbon around it was old and frayed and turning to dust like the petals. She stared at it in wonder, so fragile, so dry.

Without knowing why, she closed her fingers around the rose and felt it turn to powder in her fist. She raised her hand to her mouth and pressed her knuckles against her lips, and that is when the tears came, a hot flood that she couldn't stop. Had there been roses at the gravesite? Joel would have hated that; he never did like the sentimental things. She hadn't been able to go to the service, still recovering. There had been roses in her hospital room, the nurses saw to that. They had been white, symbols of death, and she had stared at them for weeks while her body healed and her mind refused to accept what had happened. She had watched them with dry eyes as they wilted and died in the harsh hospital lights until they were gone. By the time the lawyers came with papers and perfectly matching black pens, the roses had been replaced with fake daisies that seemed to be frozen in a posture of elation. She had stared at the fake daisies while the men talked and the day nurse paced outside in the hall. She had nodded vaguely, not knowing or caring what they were saying, aware only that she was alone and that she was trapped.

After they had gone, she turned her face away from the fake flowers and thought seriously about all the ways she might find to kill herself. Even then, she didn't cry.

The woman came to her that evening. Leslie had awoken suddenly as if pulled from sleep by invisible hands and knew instantly that she wasn't alone. At the foot of her hospital bed stood the tallest woman she had ever seen. Dressed in a severe black suit and wearing the red scarf of the Mo-tif, the woman gazed down at her in a manner that was reminiscent of the disapproving looks of the nuns from her childhood. For several moments they regarded each other in silence. It was impossible to know what the woman was thinking. Leslie wondered why it hadn't occurred to her that the Mo-tif might recruit her. Wasn't her situation almost exactly the sort that they specialized in? She didn't have to listen too closely to the lawyers to figure out that the cost of her and Joel's contract far exceeded what she would be able to earn herself.

When they had signed up four years ago, they never even considered the possibility of an accident. All they had been thinking about was earning enough to apply. It cost them almost everything and had put them into a sort of debt that was almost impossible to fathom, but they had been approved, and six months later, the baby—their baby, their Cris—had been delivered.

"You must know who I represent." The woman's voice was like the rest of her, harsh, brittle.

"You must know that they are going to blame Joel for the accident, and the cost of your original debt is going to triple because of the death of the child."

Leslie shut her eyes and turned away.

"I am here to offer you an alternative to suicide."

There was silence. The woman didn't need to say more; she hadn't needed to say even this much, and Leslie knew that all the details and the questions could come later. Right now she would accept it, her fate, her new role in society—no longer a Daughter, no longer a Bride, no longer a Mother. And with no more hope to be a Citizen.

All that was left was Wife.

She knew she should feel gratitude. An unfettered woman didn't have any options really except the Mo-tif or the Centers, and Leslie knew enough about the Centers to know that whatever the Mo-tif would offer her, she would take it. Everyone knew about the Centers, about the drugs and the chains and the forced pregnancies, the controlled air. She opened her eyes and looked unblinking at the Mo-tif woman. She nodded.

Four months later, naked and awake in the darkness, she looked at Jake, the Husband, and tried to feel something for him that wasn't anger. He had been a Groom once, she knew; he and his Bride, Angie, had probably been hopeful to someday be Parents and Citizens too. She hadn't asked. It was enough to know that Angie had died of one of the few remaining forms of cancer. Because of his loss, Jake's contract had been lessened, allowing him the ability to take a Wife. Leslie wondered if the fates had been different, if Joel would have taken a Wife to replace his lost Bride. She wondered if Joel and Angie and Cris were in the heavens like the nuns said or if they were just dirt like the dead things she found in the backyard.

She shifted against him, feeling his warmth against her skin. Had there been flowers at Angie's grave? It was something she had never thought about, but the rose haunted her thoughts. Where had it come from? From the funeral bouquets? From Angie's bridal set? Had it been a spontaneous gift from Jake—a romantic gesture?

She felt her heart begin to race again, and sweat broke out across her brow. The thought of Jake as a blushing Groom, a man in love, was foreign and yet strangely comforting. She turned onto her side and stared hard at his profile, trying to understand what it was she was suddenly feeling.

She had to risk it.

"Jake." Her voice was quiet but shockingly loud and out of context. She watched his eyes snap open. A pause, and then he looked at her.

"You okay?" The flutter in her chest kicked up a notch. There was no anger in his eyes, just sleep and mild concern.

She hesitated. They hadn't talked, she realized suddenly, really talked ever, and this was dangerous, shaky ground she was on. Her heart pounded in her chest.

"I haven't seen the stars."

She held her breath and tried to make herself small. The seconds stretched out, and she thought for a minute that he wasn't going to respond; he was just going to stare at her like she had grown another head until the sun came up. She closed her eyes; maybe she could pretend to be sleeping, having a dream. Maybe he would let it slide, this temporary bonding admission, maybe he wouldn't hold it against her. A Wife that overstepped her bounds could be returned—she knew this; it had been explained to her over and over again. A returned Wife didn't get another chance. There was a rushing of air in her ears; she felt herself at the edge of a cliff and felt faint.

His voice pulled her back. "Ever?"

Filled with shame, her eyes still closed, she whispered, "We couldn't … in the city …"

He sat up and moved away from her. She watched in fear as he fumbled for his pants, and then she hid her face when he clicked on the light and swore at the brightness.

"Well, come on then."

She looked up at him, searching his face. He stood, slightly rumpled, against the door frame, and his eyes were soft. "Here." He held out his shirt, and she pulled it on over her head unquestioningly. Barefoot and shivering, she followed him down the hall and out the back door.

She hadn't been outside at night since before Joel (women on Citizen tracks didn't risk the dangers of the night), and since becoming a Wife, she had new and more complicated rules. Leslie was filled with an overwhelming sense of recklessness. With her heart in her throat, she followed Jake carefully down the porch steps and out into the middle of the garden. When he stopped walking, she froze with her head down, trying to see the ground, her arms clutching her chest.

"Look up."

Fuzzy, tiny, cold … the stars hung above them silently. Leslie curled her toes into the dirt and gazed up, her breath ragged, her mouth open.

"I always thought I would feel better once I saw them." In the darkness, flanked by shadowy tomato plants, she felt the need to soften her voice, to murmur at barely more than a whisper. "But I just feel smaller."

"People used to think they were our ancestors." His voice was also hushed.

She shivered, and as if it were an old habit, he put his arm around her.

"The nuns told us they were angels."

"No," his voice was sharp, and even though it was still quiet, she felt the edge of anger in his words. "They're just reflections, reflections of heavenly bodies."

He dropped his arm from around her shoulders and shoved his hands into his pockets. "Long dead."

They stood in silence, almost touching, listening to the chirps of the crickets.